THE HORSESHOE TRILOGIES

Leap of Faith

by
Lucy Daniels

HYPERION
New York

Special thanks to Linda Chapman

Text copyright © 2004 by Working Partners Limited
Illustrations copyright © 2004 by Tristan Elwell

The Horseshoe Trilogies and the Volo colophon are trademarks of
Disney Enterprises, Inc.
Volo® is a registered trademark of Disney Enterprises, Inc.

Printed in the United States of America

First U.S. edition, 2004
1 3 5 7 9 10 8 6 4 2

This book is set in 12.5-point Life Roman.
ISBN 0-7868-1750-X

Visit www.hyperionbooksforchildren.com

CHAPTER ONE

Josie Grace tightened her fingers on Charity's reins. "Come on, girl," she whispered, as her eyes focused on the jump ahead.

The silver-gray mare didn't need any encouragement. Her ears pricked up and she surged forward. Sitting deep in the saddle, Josie counted the strides as the poles got closer. One, two, three . . .

Charity soared over the fence.

"Good girl!" Josie exclaimed as they landed on the short, summer grass.

Josie heard cheers from the gate. "Beautiful jump!" Jill Atterbury, one of Josie's best friends, called out.

Josie grinned and rode over to where Jill was sitting sidesaddle on her bay horse, Faith. "I think that Charity loves jumping as much as I do!"

"I want to try," Jill said, looking at the jump. "But I'll have to lower it first."

"I'll do it," Josie offered. She knew it could be difficult for Jill to get on and off with the side-saddle.

"Thanks, Josie," Jill said gratefully. The year before, Jill had been in a car accident that had left one of her hips badly damaged. She was much better now, but she was still only allowed to ride using a sidesaddle—riding normally would have put too great a strain on her weak hip.

Josie dismounted and handed Charity's reins to Jill. "How high do you want it?" she asked.

"Not too high," Jill said.

Josie nodded. Jill had only just started jumping sidesaddle. She'd had some lessons with her riding instructor and jumped a few times in the ring, but this was the first time she had jumped in the field. Josie put the ends of the poles on the ground. "How's that?"

"Fine, thanks," Jill replied.

Josie hurried back, and Jill gathered up Faith's reins. "Well, here goes."

"Don't worry. Faith will jump it easily," Josie said reassuringly, remounting Charity.

"Yes, but will I?" Jill asked. Josie knew her friend was trying to make a joke, but Josie could see that Jill's face was tense.

"You don't have to jump it," she told her friend.

"I want to," Jill said, looking at the fence with determination. She clicked her tongue and Faith walked forward. Jill touched Faith with her left heel, and the horse moved into a steady trot and then, as they reached the far corner of the field, a canter.

Josie watched Jill turn Faith toward the jump. *Go on, Jill*, she thought.

Cantering forward, Faith took off. Jill leaned forward over the high pommel of the sidesaddle and slid her hands up Faith's neck. She grabbed Faith's mane as they landed.

"Perfect!" Josie cheered.

"We did it!" Jill said in relief as she rode to the fence. Stopping beside Charity, Faith shook her long dark mane as if to say, What's all the fuss about?

"That looked really good," said Josie.

"Thanks." Jill smiled. She looked back at the jump. "It's only a small jump, though."

"So?" Josie exclaimed. "A few months ago, you'd never even ridden sidesaddle before. I think it's amazing you're jumping at all!"

Jill leaned down and hugged Faith's neck. "It's all because of Faith. She gives me confidence. I just know she'll look after me."

As if she could sense the affection in Jill's words, Faith turned her head to nuzzle Jill.

Josie felt a glow of pride. She had good reason to take a special interest in Jill's relationship with the gentle bay mare. Faith had once belonged to Josie's mom, Mary Grace. Along with Charity and Charity's mother, Hope, Mrs. Grace had used Faith to give lessons at School Farm, her old riding school. A few months before, the land the riding school was built on had been sold and Mrs. Grace had been forced to sell Faith and Hope. At first, Josie had been devastated, but it really helped knowing that Faith and Hope were both in wonderful homes. Faith had been bought by the Atterburys, and Hope now lived at a nearby center for physically challenged children.

She gave rides and was loved by all the children who came to stay there.

Jill looked at the jump. "Do you think I should try jumping higher?" she asked Josie.

"Do you want to?" Josie asked in surprise.

Jill hesitated. "I . . . I'm not sure. I sort of do, but I don't." Her fingers played in Faith's thick mane. "When I think about jumping higher I feel sick inside, but I feel stupid jumping such low fences. I used to jump much higher before my accident."

"You weren't riding sidesaddle then," Josie pointed out. "It's completely different. You shouldn't feel stupid, Jill. You've made so much progress!"

Jill didn't look convinced.

"You have," Josie insisted. "It's silly to force yourself to jump higher when you don't really want to." She grinned. "Faith and Charity already know how brave you are!"

"I guess," Jill said with a smile. "I'll call it a day for now." She patted Faith. "Do you want to turn Charity out with Faith for a while?"

Josie glanced at her watch. "No, I'd better get home. I have plans with Anna this afternoon. We're going to Lonsdale to paint the tack room.

If I don't go now, I won't have time to have lunch first."

Anna Marshall was Josie's best friend. Lonsdale was the riding school she and her twin brother, Ben, had started riding at after Mrs. Grace's school closed. The owner of Lonsdale, Sally Merton, had taught Jill to ride sidesaddle and was a good friend.

"I'll ride with you for some of the way," Jill offered. "Faith loves going out on the trails. Plus, I don't feel like getting off quite yet."

They rode to the gate and closed it carefully behind them to keep in Midnight, the big black gelding who shared the field with Faith. Jill lived on the edge of a modern housing development, but there were fields all around, and the roads were quiet.

Charity walked out with her ears forward. She was a very beautiful horse with a dapple-gray coat and a white mane and tail. She loved being ridden, but she could sometimes be unpredictable and jumpy. Now she pulled at the reins as Josie directed her to turn off the road and onto a bridle path. Josie could tell Charity wanted to canter.

"No, just walk," she told the horse. "We can canter in a while."

Josie looked over her shoulder. Faith was walking steadily a little behind them. Josie felt a rush of love for the dark bay horse. She was so sensible and good-natured. Glancing at Jill, Josie saw that her friend's brow was furrowed.

"What's wrong?" Josie asked, halting Charity and waiting for Jill to catch up.

"Nothing," Jill replied.

"Are you sure?" Josie asked as they continued along the path side by side. It wasn't like Jill to look so downcast.

Jill hesitated.

"Something's wrong," Josie said. "Come on. You can tell me."

Jill sighed. "It's the jumping. I wish I felt brave enough to jump higher fences."

"But why?" Josie asked.

"It's . . ." Jill broke off. "Oh, it doesn't matter. I'm just being silly, I guess."

"About what?" Josie felt totally clueless.

"It's my cousin," Jill admitted. "She's coming to stay with us tomorrow, with her horse."

Josie nodded. Jill had already told her that Katrina, her fourteen-year-old cousin, was going to be staying with the Atterburys for a month. Katrina's mom and dad were going to Australia on business, and Katrina didn't want to go with them because she'd have missed a big horse show.

"Katrina has qualified Flight for the regional finals of her class. If she does well there, she'll qualify for the national finals in October," Jill added.

Josie nodded. "What's that got to do with your jumping Faith?"

Jill swallowed. "Two years ago I went to stay with Katrina and we had a great time. I took Marmalade—you know, my old horse—with me. I was only nine, but we did lots of jumping—even some really high jumps. I . . . I don't know what she'll think of me if I can't do that now."

"She'll understand," Josie tried to reassure her. "I'm sure she will. She knows about your accident."

"I know. It's just, well . . . Katrina's so brave. She's not scared of anything." Jill anxiously bit her lip. "I'm worried she's going to think I'm a coward."

"That's ridiculous!" Josie exclaimed. "There's no way Katrina's going to think that. I bet she's really going to respect you for being brave enough to start riding again."

"Do you think so?" Jill asked.

"Yes! So what if you're only jumping small jumps right now?" Josie said. "You'll be jumping higher soon. You've just got to do things when you feel ready."

"That's what Sally's been saying," Jill admitted. "She's always telling me I've got to take things slowly." She sighed. "I suppose I am just being silly. Even if Katrina and I can't jump together like we did last time, we can still have fun."

"Of course you can," Josie told her. "You can go on trail rides and you can jump—just not so high."

Jill looked happier. "You're right. It'll be fine, won't it?"

Josie smiled. "Of course it will."

"Thanks, Josie," Jill said gratefully. "I feel better now. I can't wait for you to meet Katrina. You'll really like her." Her eyes lit up with a sudden idea. "Why don't you come over in the morning? She's coming at eleven."

"Okay," Josie agreed. Charity pulled at her bit and shook her head. "I think Charity wants to canter," Josie said, looking at the grassy path ahead of them.

"That's fine by me," Jill grinned. She clicked her tongue. "Bet you can't catch us!" she called out over her shoulder as Faith surged forward.

Charity plunged in excitement at the prospect of a race. Loosening her reins, Josie laughed and let the gray horse go. Within a few strides they had caught up with Faith. Side by side the two horses galloped up the hill, their tails streaming out behind them.

After lunch, Josie went up to her room to read her newest horse magazine. A little while later, she heard voices from downstairs. Then her mom's voice reached her.

"Josie! Anna's here!" Mrs. Grace called up the stairs.

Josie had lost track of time. Quickly, she tried to drag a brush through her unruly hair. Grabbing a ponytail holder, she tied her thick, auburn waves back. "Come on, Basil—downstairs," she said. Basil, a brown-and-white terrier, was lying in a patch of sun. Josie loved her attic bedroom. It had sloping ceilings and varnished floorboards hidden under a multicolored rug. The white walls were covered with horse posters, and the big windows looked out over the garden with its wonderful wilderness of shrubs and overgrown flower beds. Beyond the garden lay Charity's field. Josie loved being able to keep an eye on her just by looking outside. Even though the horse was living on her neighbor's property, Josie could still see her.

Basil scampered to the door as if he had been expecting a walk. "Sorry, boy," Josie said as she followed him down the winding staircase, "but I can't take you out with me today."

Mrs. Grace was waiting at the bottom of the staircase. "Don't worry," she called, overhearing Josie's words to Basil. "I'll take him out for a W . . . A . . . L . . . K when you're gone."

Basil spun around, barking in excitement.

Josie grinned. "And you thought Basil couldn't spell, Mom."

Mrs. Grace shook her head. "That dog is far too clever for his own good!" She opened the door. "Go on, don't keep the Marshalls waiting."

"Bye, Mom!" Josie called, hurrying out the door.

Anna was sitting in the car with her twin brother, Ben, and their mom, Lynne Marshall. "Come on,

Josie!" she called through the open window. "We've been waiting for ages."

"Anna's exaggerating, as usual," said Mrs. Marshall as Josie squeezed into the car. "We've only been here a minute."

"It feels like forever," Anna said, her brown eyes impatient. "I want to get to Lonsdale Stables. We're going to take everything out of the tack room, fix it all up, paint the walls—and clean all the tack!"

Ben raised his eyebrows. "You have a very weird idea of a good time, Anna."

"It's better than just being plain weird, like you," Anna retorted, grinning. She jumped out of the way as her brother aimed a punch at her arm.

"Enough!" their mother said from the front.

Anna turned to Josie. "It'll be fun, won't it?"

Josie nodded. She liked going to Lonsdale Stables, and redecorating the tack room there sounded like a great way to spend an afternoon. Josie loved everything to do with horses. "So, you're not going to help?" she asked Ben.

He shrugged. "I suppose I might as well," he sighed.

Josie smiled to herself. She knew that, deep down, Ben was probably looking forward to it just as much, but that he wouldn't show it openly, as Anna had. The two of them might have looked very similar—they both had the same dark hair and olive skin, inherited from their father—but they couldn't have been more different in personality. Anna always said what she thought, and she never seemed to stop talking. Ben, on the other hand, was far quieter and much more reserved. Josie was good friends with them both.

As soon as they reached the stables, Anna jumped out. "Come on! Let's go and get started."

As the friends cleaned the tack room, Josie told Anna about Jill's cousin.

"Do you think she loves horses as much as we do?" Anna asked.

"If she is Jill's cousin, I'm sure she does!" Josie said. She smiled. This week was going to be so much fun—she just knew it.

CHAPTER TWO

"They're here!" Jill exclaimed the next morning, as a blue car pulled into her driveway. "That's Aunt Rachel and Uncle Andrew's car." She hurried to the driveway and waved excitedly.

Josie jumped down off the gate and looked at the car. It was pulling a matching blue horse trailer. As it stopped, a horse whinnied inside, and there was the sound of hooves stamping on the trailer floor. The car doors opened, and Jill's aunt, uncle, and cousin got out.

"Jill!" her aunt exclaimed, hugging her. "You look wonderful! How are you?"

"I'm fine, Aunt Rachel," Jill replied.

Josie looked at Katrina. She had straight, dark, shoulder-length hair like Jill's, but her face was very different. Jill's face was thin, and she had large, brown eyes. But Katrina, Josie noticed as she neared the group, had a round face, green eyes, and freckles on her nose and cheeks. She grinned at Jill. "Hi, there, stranger. It's been ages since I saw you." She looked curiously in Josie's direction.

"This is Josie Grace," Jill explained. "My new horse, Faith, used to belong to Josie's mom. Josie, this is Katrina and my aunt and uncle, Rachel and Andrew Stevenson."

The Stevensons all smiled at Josie. "Pleased to meet you, Josie," Mrs. Stevenson said.

"Is that your new horse?" Katrina asked, looking at Faith, who was grazing beside Charity in the field.

Jill nodded. "Yes, that's Faith. What do you think of her?"

"She's perfect," said Katrina. "I love dark bays, and she's got a very pretty head."

Seeing Jill's eyes shining with delight, Josie felt a rush of relief. Katrina seemed really nice. Now she was sure Jill had been worrying for nothing.

Just then, Jill's mom and dad came out of the house. "Hello there!" Mrs. Atterbury called as they hurried over to say hi.

As the families greeted each other, the horse inside the trailer whinnied again and stamped its hoof.

"Dad, we should probably get Flight out," said Katrina, turning toward the trailer.

Her father nodded. "He can be a bit of a handful," he warned everyone. "So I'd stand out of the way."

Katrina got into the trailer through the side door and after a minute shouted, "Ready, Dad!"

Josie watched curiously as Mr. Stevenson lowered the ramp. There was a loud snort, and a bright chestnut horse in a navy sheet backed out quickly.

"Steady, boy, steady," Katrina said soothingly, hanging on to the lead rope.

The horse looked around, the veins standing out on his sleek chestnut neck. *He's gorgeous*, Josie thought admiringly. His head was fine, like a thoroughbred's, and he had two white socks, and in the center of his forehead there was a tiny, white star. He whirled around, his dark eyes excited.

"Mom, can you help me take his shipping wraps off?" Katrina asked.

Mrs. Stevenson made her way over to the horse and quickly began to unravel the navy shipping bandages wrapped around Flight's legs. Flight snorted and sidestepped.

"He looks like a lively guy," Mr. Atterbury commented.

Katrina stroked Flight's cheek as he shook his head. "Steady, boy," she said. The horse impatiently shoved her hand away with his nose.

"All done," Mrs. Stevenson said, pulling off the last wrap.

"I'll walk him up the road," said Katrina. "It'll help calm him down."

"Katrina seems very confident with him," Jill's mother remarked as Katrina led Flight away.

"She is," Mrs. Stevenson replied with a smile. "But then, you know what Katrina's like—she's never scared of anything."

"Come inside," said Mr. Atterbury to the Stevensons. He looked at Jill and Josie. "Are you two coming in, or are you going to stay out here with Katrina?"

"We'll stay here," Jill replied. "I'll show Katrina where to put all of Flight's stuff."

"I think she's going to find it strange looking after him all by herself," Mr. Stevenson commented. "We keep him on full board at home—Katrina doesn't have time to muck out the stall and feed him, what with her schoolwork during the week and shows on weekends." He smiled. "I think she's going to find it rather a shock this month." He followed the other adults inside.

"Wouldn't it be strange having a horse on full board?" Jill said quietly as she and Josie watched Katrina lead Flight down the road. "Paying somebody else to do all your work and take care of your horse?"

Josie nodded. She couldn't imagine having someone else looking after Charity every day. It would be weird—no cleaning up or grooming, just riding. "I wouldn't like it," she said.

"Me, neither," Jill agreed. "I love looking after Faith." Her eyes turned back toward Flight. He was pulling against the lead rope, but Katrina managed to keep him under control. "What do you think of Flight, Josie?"

"He's absolutely beautiful," Josie said. She admired the athletic way he moved, the curve of his neck, and the perfect lines of his head.

"I think I might tack him up," Katrina said as she approached them. "If I ride him around, maybe he'll calm down a bit. Could you do me a favor, Jill, and grab my tack from the trailer, please?"

"Sure," Jill replied.

"I'll help," Josie offered. They grabbed the saddle and bridle and brought them back to Katrina. It wasn't easy to get the tack on with Flight moving restlessly, but finally he was ready.

"Thanks." Katrina smiled at Josie and Jill.

Flight pranced around the field with his tail held up like an amber flag. Every few strides, he shied, as if he saw monsters hiding behind the bushes. Josie and Jill sat on the fence and watched.

"He sure doesn't look 'push-button,'" Josie said to Jill. "He makes Katrina work."

Jill nodded. "I'm glad Faith's calmer."

"Katrina's a really good rider, though," Josie commented, looking at Katrina's light hands and secure seat that hardly moved in the saddle as Flight spooked and danced.

Katrina urged Flight into a trot and then, a while later, a canter. Gradually he seemed to settle down.

After fifteen minutes, she rode over to the fence. "Do you think you could put a cross-rail up for me and put a pole between those barrels, please?"

"You're going to jump him?" Josie said, a bit shocked.

"It'll calm him down," Katrina replied.

Josie was surprised. Flight had only just arrived. If it had been her horse, she would have let him settle in for a few days before jumping him. Still, she thought with a shrug, Katrina obviously knows her own horse best.

She went with Jill to put up the jumps. After they had moved out of the way, Katrina picked up a canter and turned Flight toward the cross-rail. Seeing the jump, he threw up his head and snatched at the reins. Katrina didn't try to restrain him. Sitting confidently in the saddle, she rode him boldly up to the fence. As he flung himself over, her body moved with his, and they flew over it.

"They're good, aren't they?" Josie remarked.

Jill nodded. Katrina jumped the slightly higher vertical and cantered over to the gate.

"He's a fantastic jumper!" Josie called to her.

Katrina looked pleased. "He is, isn't he? I'm jumping him three-six at home."

"Wow!" Josie was very impressed. The highest she'd ever jumped was three feet, and that had been pretty scary. Three foot, six inches seemed huge!

Jill stroked Flight's nose. "You're a very special boy, aren't you?"

"Would you like a turn on him, Jill?" Katrina asked.

"I can't," Jill replied reluctantly. "Because of the accident, I can only ride sidesaddle."

Katrina nodded understandingly and looked at Josie. "How about you, Josie?" she offered. "Would you like to ride him?"

"I'd love to!" Josie answered eagerly.

"Great." Katrina dismounted and gave Josie her helmet. "Just start with a walk and trot. He can be quite difficult."

Josie swung herself lightly into the saddle.

Almost immediately, Flight moved forward. "Easy, now," Josie said soothingly. Gathering the reins, she let him walk on. His strides were short and fast. Josie felt as though he might explode from underneath her at any moment. She patted his neck and talked softly to him. He made Charity seem positively quiet.

Josie eased Flight into a trot. He tried to break into a canter, but she gently held him back. He shook his head and slowed down. Concentrating hard, Josie rode him in a circle, moving him from a trot to a walk and back to a trot. After five minutes, he started to lower his head and relax into the bit.

"You're doing great," Katrina said, as Josie trotted past the gate.

Josie smoothly halted Flight. "Thanks," she said with a smile.

"Do you want to try a jump?" Katrina asked. "You can if you want."

"I'd love to!" Josie replied.

Katrina went over and stood near the cross-rail. "Try this one first. Just let him go at his own speed, and go with him. If you try and slow him down, he'll just go faster," she warned.

Josie nodded and gave Flight a nudge with her heel. He sprang into a canter at once. "Steady, boy," she said, sitting deep in the saddle and closing her fingers gently on the reins. He slowed slightly, and she turned him toward the fence. Remembering what Katrina had said, Josie sat still in the saddle and let him go. Reaching the fence, she leaned forward and Flight flew over the poles.

"Gosh!" Josie gasped, struggling to pull him up afterward. "He really likes to go fast, doesn't he?"

Katrina smiled. "You should see him in a jump-off!" She looked at the other jump, still set high from when she had jumped it. "Bet you wouldn't jump that on him."

"Bet I would!" Josie grinned. Every nerve in her body felt as though it were buzzing with adrenaline. She'd never jumped a horse like Flight!

"Go on, then," Katrina said.

"Really?" Josie asked.

Katrina nodded. Josie shortened her reins and headed toward the jump. It was high—nearly three foot three. Flight's ears pricked up, he increased his speed, and the next second, he was flying through the air.

Josie had to circle Flight three times before she could get him under control enough to stop. "Wow!" she said breathlessly, finally pulling to a halt. Her fingers were red and sore from the reins, and she could feel her heart pounding against her chest.

"Well done!" Katrina called. "I thought you'd chicken out! Most people are too scared to jump him that high. Want me to put it up some more?"

Josie glanced at the fence, where Jill was standing by herself. "It's all right," she said, suddenly worried that Jill might be feeling left out. "I'll stop now." She patted Flight's sweaty neck. "He's really hot. Why don't we all go out for a hack? It'll help cool him down."

Katrina shrugged. "I guess he has done enough jumping for today."

They walked back over to the fence.

"That was awesome!" Jill said. "Are you going to jump him again, Josie?"

Josie shook her head. "I thought we could all go out for a hack instead—if you want to."

Jill nodded. "Definitely."

She and Josie quickly tacked up, and ten minutes later they were ready. Charity and Faith walked side by side while Flight pranced and pulled up ahead of them.

Katrina looked over her shoulder. "Do you live nearby?" she asked Josie.

"On the other side of town," Josie answered. "It's about a half-hour ride away. But it's mainly across fields, so it's not too bad. I come to see Jill a lot."

"Are there many good trails around here?" Katrina asked.

Josie nodded. "Lots."

"We could go for a ride together tomorrow," Jill suggested. "In the woods there are logs to jump and great hills to race up and down."

"And, if it's sunny we could have a picnic," Josie suggested. "We could ride down to the river and eat there."

"Definitely! What do you think, Katrina?" Jill asked, looking at her cousin.

Katrina grinned. "I think I'm going to like staying here."

Later that night, Josie told her mom and dad about Katrina as she helped set the table for dinner. "She's nice, and Flight, her horse, is unbelievable."

Mr. Grace stirred a pot of pasta sauce on the stove. "Did you ride him?"

"Uh-huh," Josie replied. "I jumped him. The fence was huge—almost three-three." Her eyes glowed as she relived the moment. "It was so amazing!"

Mrs. Grace paused in the middle of taking some plates out of the cabinet, and frowned. "You *jumped* him?"

Josie guessed what her mom was thinking. "I know. It was a bit strange to jump him when he'd just arrived, but Katrina said it would calm him down—and she was right," she added in Katrina's defense. "He was much more relaxed after he'd been ridden."

"Even so," Mary Grace said, "I'm not sure jumping him was the most sensible thing to do. His legs were probably stiff after the trip. Taking him out for a quiet hack might have been the better option."

"We went out for a hack, too," Josie said. "And we're going out again tomorrow, for a picnic ride to the river."

Mr. Grace carried a steaming pot of spaghetti over to the sink to drain it. "So the summer plans are looking up, after all?" he smiled.

"By the way," said her mom, putting the salad on the table. "Anna called earlier. She's going to

Friendship House with her mom at three o'clock tomorrow afternoon. She was calling to ask if you wanted to go and see Hope with her. I said you'd call her back."

Josie jumped up. "I'll call her now. Can I go after the picnic?"

Her mom nodded.

"Don't be long," her dad warned as she hurried to the door. "Dinner's almost ready."

"I won't," Josie promised. "I'm starving."

She picked up the phone in the hallway and quickly dialed Anna's number. Her friend answered.

"Hi, it's me," said Josie. "I got your message. I'd love to come."

"Cool," Anna replied. "Mom said we can pick you up on the way. Ben's not coming with us—he's staying at his friend Zach's. It will be great to go. It seems like ages since I saw Hope."

"It hasn't been that long," Josie said, grinning.

"Still, it seems like forever. I used to see her almost every day at School Farm," Anna gently reminded her.

"I know," Josie said understandingly. Hope was the horse Anna had always ridden at School Farm, and Josie knew her friend missed her most, out of all the horses.

"Anyway, how was this morning?" Anna asked. "Did you meet Jill's cousin?"

"Yes," Josie replied. "She even let me ride her horse, Flight. I jumped him almost three-three!"

"Wow!" said Anna, impressed.

"And she was really nice to Jill," Josie went on. "I think they're going to get along great."

"Josie! Dinner's ready!" Mr. Grace called.

"I've got to go," Josie said quickly. "I'll see you tomorrow afternoon."

"Bye!" said Anna.

Josie put the phone down. She couldn't wait for the next day—a picnic ride and then a chance to see sweet Hope. What could be better than that?

CHAPTER THREE

The sun shone brightly as Josie rode Charity to Jill's house the next morning. It was the perfect day for a picnic and ride—blue skies, white clouds, and a light breeze. Charity trotted eagerly, the saddlebag containing Josie's lunch bouncing gently with each stride.

Jill was grooming Faith in the field when Josie arrived. "Hi!" she called.

Faith and Charity nickered to each other. Josie grinned. "Faith looks like she's been having a mud bath!"

"She managed to find the one muddy spot left in

the field and roll in it," Jill said. "Typical!" She swept the brush over Faith's coat and sneezed as a cloud of dust flew up into the air.

"Here, I'll give you a hand," Josie offered. She loosened Charity's girth and tied her up to the fence using a spare halter that Jill always kept out for the times when Josie rode over.

"Were you just trying to make work for Jill?" she said to Faith as she picked up a stiff brush. Faith lifted her nose and nuzzled Josie's forehead with her soft lips.

"I love the way she kisses like that," Jill smiled.

"Me, too," said Josie, rubbing Faith's forehead. "You're just a big softy, aren't you, girl?" Faith snorted, and Josie began to brush the dust out of Faith's tangled mane. "Where's Katrina?" she asked. She could see Flight grazing by Midnight under one of the trees halfway down the field. He was wearing a lightweight, silver turnout sheet and a fly mask.

"She's inside," Jill said. "She was still in bed when I came out to get ready."

"In bed?" Josie repeated.

"She says she always sleeps in during the summer," Jill said.

Josie frowned. "But we're going for our ride at eleven. If she doesn't get up soon, she won't have time to groom Flight."

As she spoke, the back door opened and Katrina walked out. "Hi," she called. She grabbed a lead from the shed that doubled as the tack room and walked down the field to get Flight. "Come on, Flight!" The chestnut horse's ears flickered, but he didn't look up.

Josie frowned in surprise. Faith, Hope, and Charity usually all whinnied in greeting and would come trotting over with their ears pricked. But Flight didn't move toward Katrina. She had to walk over to him to clip his lead on. Giving him a quick pat, she led him up to the fence.

"Are you almost ready?" Katrina asked Jill, as she tied her horse up beside Faith.

"Not quite," said Jill. "But by the time you've groomed Flight, I will be."

"Oh, I don't usually bother with grooming." Katrina started to pull off Flight's sheet.

Josie and Jill both stared at her. "You don't groom him?" Josie echoed.

Katrina shook her head. "I just brush any muddy

bits off his neck and legs and tack him up. The sheet keeps the rest of him clean."

"But . . . but, grooming's fun," said Jill.

Katrina threw the rug over the fence. "It's not my sort of thing. The grooms at the stables usually brush him, and I always bathe him before a show. That's all he needs. But don't worry, I'll ride him around the field while you finish grooming your horses, and then, when you're ready, we can head out."

Not waiting for an answer, she walked to the shed to fetch Flight's tack. Josie stared after her in astonishment. She loved grooming Charity. Sometimes Charity would rest her muzzle on Josie's shoulder as she worked, and other times she would just doze with her eyes half closed. Josie couldn't imagine not doing that on a daily basis.

Katrina returned with Flight's tack. Sweeping the body brush over Faith's dark coat, Josie saw Flight fidget as Katrina tacked him up.

When Katrina put his saddle on, he shifted first to one side and then the other. "Stand still!" Katrina said sharply.

"Is he always this wired?" asked Josie, going over to hold him for Katrina while she mounted.

"He's always lively, but he's worse when he's in a new place," Katrina said, putting on her helmet. "It can be a nightmare at shows. We always end up in the warm-up ring for a while." She patted Flight, but he hardly seemed to notice. "It's just his breeding. He's half thoroughbred, and thoroughbreds tend to be really excitable."

Not all of them, thought Josie, looking at where Midnight was grazing quietly under the tree and thinking about Connie, the thoroughbred mare her mom sometimes rode.

Katrina swung herself onto Flight's back. The horse plunged forward, almost knocking Josie over. "Sorry," said Katrina. She touched Flight's neck. "Come on, then, let's go do some work."

Flight trotted away.

"I'm glad Faith's not like that," Jill said, after Katrina left. "You'd never be able to relax."

Josie nodded and walked over to her gray mare. "You're just enough for me," she said. Charity pushed her head against her lovingly and Josie rubbed her ears. *No*, she thought happily, *I wouldn't swap Charity for anything.*

* * *

"Are you all set?" asked Katrina when Josie and Jill finally mounted. She had been jumping Flight, and his chestnut coat was damp with sweat.

"Ready," Jill said, patting Faith's neck.

As the three girls rode along the path, Josie asked Katrina how the jumping had gone.

"Flight did okay," Katrina said. "But I wasn't jumping very high. Tomorrow I'm going to put the fences up and get some serious schooling in."

"They looked pretty high to me already," Jill said.

They turned off the road and headed in to the cool shade of the woods. The long, sandy track stretched out in front of them—straight, wide, and inviting. "Let's canter!" Katrina said eagerly.

Josie and Jill didn't need any persuading. Flight leaped forward and Charity and Faith raced after him. It felt wonderful to thunder along the sand together.

"We'd better stop here," Josie shouted as the track began to narrow. They slowed down. The horses were all breathing hard, but their ears were pricked, and even sensible Faith was pulling at her reins.

"That was great!" Jill laughed.

"Charity loved it," Josie agreed.

"Look, there's a fallen log." Katrina pointed through the trees to another path that had a small log lying across it. "Anybody want to jump it?"

Josie looked questioningly at Jill.

Jill's jaw set in a determined line. "Okay," she said.

Katrina set off.

"Are you sure?" Josie asked Jill as she turned Charity around. The mare was eager to follow Flight.

Jill nodded, so Josie let Charity go. The gray horse flew over the log with a huge leap. Josie pulled her up just in time to see Faith jumping safely over it, Jill holding on to her mane.

Katrina barely paused on Flight. "Now let's go down that hill!" she shouted, seeing a dip in the track in front of them. Not waiting for them to reply, she headed off at a gallop.

"Are you up for this?" Josie quickly asked Jill.

"Yes—but definitely not at a gallop!" Jill said.

"We can just trot down it," Josie told her.

"This is so cool!" Katrina exclaimed, as they came to a halt beside her. She looked around. "Next we can jump that bush over there."

"I think I'll just walk for a while," Josie replied, patting Charity's warm neck.

"Me, too," Jill agreed. "Faith's already sweating, and I thought we were just going on a quiet hack."

"Well then, I'll catch up with you when I've jumped it," Katrina said, and she cantered Flight away toward the bush.

The chestnut horse soared over the bush, and then Katrina galloped him down a very steep bank.

"She's wild, isn't she?" Jill said admiringly. "I would never go down something as steep as that—not even at a walk!"

"She doesn't seem scared of anything," Josie agreed, watching Flight scramble up the other side. "But I'm not sure that is always a good thing."

They reached a fork in the path. "Which way do we go?" Katrina asked, cantering up to them.

"Left," Josie said. "The right path leads to the river, too, but then we'd have to go on the roads, and it's much slower that way."

They continued to trot down the path. Suddenly Josie pulled Charity back to a walk. A tree had fallen across the path, and even at its lowest point it still looked very wide *and* very intimidating.

"Oh, no," Josie said. "I didn't know this was here. I guess we'd better go around on the roads after all."

"Why? It looks like it'll be fun to jump!" Katrina said, riding past her.

Urging Flight forward, she galloped toward the tree trunk and disappeared over it in a flurry of sand and leaves.

Charity plunged in excitement and Josie only just managed to stop her from following Flight over the tree. "Steady, girl, steady." Struggling to get Charity under control, she glanced over at Jill with concern. "What do you want to do?"

"I don't want to jump it," Jill said, her face pale. "It's way too big, Josie."

"Don't worry," said Josie. "We can go around by the road if you want."

"But what about Katrina?"

"I'll go after her and tell her to come back," Josie said.

Just then, Katrina reappeared, jumping back over the tree trunk. "What's keeping the two of you?" she demanded, pulling Flight up beside them.

Josie glanced at Jill.

Jill blushed. "I . . . I don't want to jump the log, Katrina. It's too high for me."

"All right," Katrina said. "We can go around by the road if you want."

"You really don't mind?" Jill said, looking up uncertainly.

"Well," Katrina replied, "it's okay."

Jill looked relieved.

They went back to the fork in the trail and took the path that led to the road. They rode along and chatted quietly.

"This is boring!" Katrina exclaimed. "Come on, let's do some more cantering."

"Not here," Josie warned her. "The track gets narrow around the next corner and there's a really steep drop to the left. We can canter after that."

Katrina shrugged and walked Flight along the narrow section of path. Josie and Jill followed.

By the time they reached the river, the horses were tired, and even Flight seemed content to stand quietly in the shade while Josie, Jill, and Katrina sat on the riverbank and ate their lunch.

"This is perfect," Jill said, munching on a tuna

sandwich. They had taken off their riding boots and were dangling their feet in the cool water.

"I love summer," said Josie, taking a huge bite out of her ham-and-cheese sandwich.

"Mmmm," Katrina agreed. "We should do this again."

Jill smiled at Katrina. "Definitely!"

"Are you going to come and watch me jump Flight in the field tomorrow morning?" Katrina asked Josie. "I'm going to put the jumps up."

Josie nodded. She didn't have anything else planned.

"Then you'll really get to see how good Flight is," Katrina grinned at her.

As they finished their lunch, Josie sighed. "I'm stuffed!" she said, leaning back in the grass.

"Me, too," said Jill.

Josie looked at Charity. The horse had gotten sweaty on the ride over and the sweat had dried in long streaks. "I think I might wash Charity down," she said. With a groan, she got to her feet.

"Good idea," Jill said, standing up, too. "Are you going to wash Flight, Katrina?"

"I'm too full to move," Katrina answered, closing

her eyes and lying back in the sun. "He'll be fine."

Josie frowned. Flight was the sweatiest of the three horses. But what could she say? Katrina had her eyes closed and didn't seem bothered by it.

Josie walked over to the horses with Jill and they led Faith and Charity to the river. Scooping up handfuls of cool water, they washed the sweat away. Flight watched them with a curious expression on his face.

Josie hated seeing the streaks of sweat on him. "Katrina, would you mind if we washed Flight down?" she asked.

"If you want," Katrina mumbled, sounding half asleep.

Josie tied Charity up again and led Flight down to the water. At first he jumped back in surprise when Jill splashed water over him, but Josie stroked him, and he quickly calmed down.

"I think he likes it," said Jill, sounding pleased.

Josie nodded. She couldn't believe that Katrina wasn't bathing him herself. Josie couldn't get used to Katrina's seeming lack of interest in doing anything with Flight apart from riding him. It was beginning to bother her.

After the horses had dried off in the sun's heat, the girls repacked their saddlebags and got back on.

"I'll ride back part of the way with you and then head home," Josie said.

Within minutes Katrina was cantering off down the path to jump logs and bushes. Charity, refreshed after her rest, pulled on the reins, eager to catch up with Flight. Josie couldn't help feeling relieved when they reached the path she needed to take to get home. "Will you be fine with Katrina if I go now?" Josie whispered to Jill.

"Yes, Faith's being as good as ever," Jill said, patting the bay horse's neck. "You go."

"See you tomorrow!" Josie called to Katrina, who was heading off down a bank.

"Yeah!" Katrina waved. "You'll be able to see some real jumping then!"

CHAPTER
FOUR

"How was the picnic?" Anna asked Josie as Mrs. Marshall drove them over to Friendship House later that afternoon.

"Great," replied Josie. "We were out for a while, and Katrina galloped Flight up and down all the banks."

"So what's she like?" Anna asked curiously.

Josie hesitated. "She's nice, but . . . well, she doesn't look after Flight that well. She hardly ever grooms him, and after lunch, she couldn't even be bothered to wash him down when we got to the river. Jill and I had to do it."

Anna frowned. "I don't think I like her," she said in her usual blunt way.

"But she's a lot of fun," Josie put in quickly, not wanting Anna to get the wrong impression of Katrina. "And she's an amazing rider." It was hard to explain. Normally she wouldn't ever be friends with someone who wasn't interested in looking after her horse properly, but she liked Katrina. "You'll have to meet her. You could come over to Jill's with me one day or—" She had a sudden idea. "We could go swimming together or something."

Anna's mom looked over her shoulder. "The outdoor swimming pool at Barnston Hall is open for the summer. I don't mind driving you all over there one afternoon when I'm not working."

"That would be great!" said Anna, looking at Josie, who nodded eagerly. The pool at Barnston Hall was really fun. There was a diving board and an ice-cream stand and lots of places to lie down and soak up the sun.

"How about tomorrow?" Mrs. Marshall asked.

"I'll call Jill tonight and see if she and Katrina want to come," Josie said. "It will be great!"

Mrs. Marshall turned in to the driveway of

Friendship House. It was a large, honey-colored building with gardens and green grass all around it.

"I'll see you back here at six when you've finished visiting Hope," Anna's mom said.

"Sounds good," said Anna.

"See you later," Josie called to Mrs. Marshall as the girls hurried around the side of the house.

"I wonder if Zoe will be here," Josie said.

Zoe was the cook's granddaughter, and she also helped look after Hope. When Josie and Anna had first met Zoe, the girl had been a bit standoffish. It had taken awhile, but now they all got along really well.

"There she is!" Anna pointed to the pasture.

A girl with blond hair was leading a gray horse up and down the field. A little boy was riding, and in the shade of a massive oak tree, three other children waited with an adult.

"Hi, Zoe!" Josie called.

Zoe waved, and, as Josie and Anna jogged toward the pasture gate, the gray horse lifted her head and whinnied. Josie smiled. Even she had to admit that Hope wasn't the prettiest horse in the world—but she was the kindest, gentlest horse imaginable. And it was clear from the happy expressions on the children's faces that they loved her.

"Hi, there," Zoe said as Josie and Anna reached her. "I didn't know you two were coming."

Hope nudged at Josie's hands. Josie fed her a peppermint from her pocket. "Anna's mom brought us over," she told Zoe. "We thought we'd come and see you and Hope and then help Lynne with some of the painting."

The little boy riding Hope looked curiously at her. "My name's Alex."

"Hi, I'm Josie," she said.

"And I'm Anna," Anna added.

"Alex loves Hope. Don't you, Alex?" said Zoe.

Alex nodded and patted Hope's solid neck. "I wish I could ride her all the time."

Josie smiled. She missed having Hope at home, but it was wonderful knowing that the horse was making so many children happy.

"Tell you what," Zoe said to Alex. "When you've finished riding her, how about we take her back to the stable, and you can help me wash her tail and legs? We can make her look really beautiful."

Alex nodded eagerly. "Yes, please."

Zoe looked at Josie and Anna. "Do you two want to help?"

"Of course," Josie grinned.

By four o'clock, Hope was spotlessly clean. Her coat had been brushed, and her newly washed tail and legs were the color of fresh snow.

"All done," said Anna, painting on a last coat of hoof oil. The hoof oil not only strengthened Hope's hooves but also made them very shiny.

"Perfect," Josie said.

"She looks really nice," Alex agreed.

"Just wait," Zoe grinned. "I bet she rolls in the mud as soon as we put her out in the field."

"That's the trouble with gray horses—they never stay clean for long," Josie sighed.

"I don't mind. I really like brushing her," said Alex. "Can I help you tomorrow, please, Zoe?"

She smiled at him. "Of course."

Josie glanced at her watch. "Should we go and see if your mom needs some help?" she asked Anna.

"Probably," Anna replied.

"I'll see you later," Zoe told them.

Saying good-bye to Hope, Zoe, and Alex, Josie

and Anna made their way to the main house. As they drew nearer, they heard loud shrieks and squeals coming from the patio area.

"Something sure sounds like fun," Anna said, exchanging looks with Josie.

"Oh, wow!" Josie exclaimed when they turned the corner.

A group of eight children were running around on a giant piece of white canvas that was taped to the patio. There were trays of red, blue, green, and yellow paint all around the outside of the canvas. The children were dipping their feet and hands in the paint and then making footprints and handprints on the canvas. There was paint everywhere.

Mrs. Marshall was shouting out warnings as she refilled a tray with blue paint. "Don't taste it, Sasha! Mark, you've got it in your hair! Nathan, please, stay on the canvas!" Catching sight of Anna and Josie, she looked relieved. "Have you come to join the chaos? I could certainly use a hand."

"It looks pretty messy!" said Anna.

"But fun," Josie grinned. She sat down on the ground and began to pull off her sneakers. "What can we do to help?"

"Just generally supervise," replied Mrs. Marshall, as a little boy made a dash for the lawn. "Nathan! No!" She shook her head despairingly. "And to think that last night this seemed like a good idea! There're going to be footprints all over the grass! Can you help me keep the children on the canvas?"

Josie and Anna herded the escaping children back onto the canvas. The kids squealed and laughed as they ran to the trays and plunged their hands and feet into the bright paint.

Anna grinned at her mom. "It may be messy, but they're all having a great time, Mom."

Mrs. Marshall looked around at the happy children and smiled. "I guess they are." She headed to the center of the mat, where there was an expanse of canvas that hadn't been painted yet. "Over here," she called to the children. "This part needs doing next."

Looking at the tray of blue paint, Josie couldn't resist dipping her feet into it.

"It's so cold!" she gasped as the thick paint squelched over her toes. She quickly stepped out, making two blue footprints on the mat.

"I want to try," said Anna. She dipped her hands in and made a circle of handprints.

"Very artistic," Josie teased.

"Not as artistic as this!" Anna grinned, and, running forward, she planted a huge handprint on Josie's back.

"Anna!" Josie cried. "Oh, you asked for it!"

Anna turned to run, but her foot slipped, and the next minute she was sprawling on the canvas. She gasped and sat up. Her arms, T-shirt, and jeans were all covered in paint. "Look at me!" she cried.

The children standing around her squealed and pointed at her, smiles on their faces.

Josie was laughing so hard she couldn't stand up.

"Josie! Anna!"

They swung around guiltily. Anna's mom was staring at them in horror.

"I'm sorry, Mom. I slipped!" Anna stood up sheepishly, wiping her hands on her jeans. She was covered in paint from head to toe.

"You're supposed to be supervising," her mother said, but, to Josie's relief, the corners of Mrs. Marshall's mouth began to twitch. She shook her head and smiled. "Look at the two of you! Anna, you've got paint all over you!"

Anna grinned at her. "At least I didn't get it on the grass, Mom!"

By six o'clock, Josie and Anna were walking to the car, exhausted and covered in paint.

"I think I'd better put some towels down for you to sit on," Mrs. Marshall said, looking at their paint-spattered clothes. She sighed. "Your jeans are never going to be the same again."

"I don't mind!" Josie said. "It was fun."

"The kids really enjoyed it, too," said Anna. "Did you see how proud they were when they saw the canvas at the end?"

Mrs. Marshall nodded. "It was a real success, wasn't it?"

"If you want to do it again, I'll help," Josie offered eagerly.

"Me, too," Anna agreed.

"Thank you," Mrs. Marshall said, smiling as she unlocked the car and looked at the paint-soaked girls. "But somehow I think it's going to be a while before I try that idea again!"

When Josie arrived at Jill's the next morning, Katrina

was putting up a course of jumps. "They're so high!" Josie exclaimed, leading Charity into the field.

Katrina laughed. "These are little!" She looked around. "I think I'll put them up another hole." She raised the metal cup. "Are you going to jump Charity?"

Josie shook her head. After the long ride the day before, she felt Charity deserved an easy day.

Jill waved from the fence. Faith whinnied and Josie led Charity over to say hello. As the two horses touched noses, Jill helped Josie untack. "Those jumps are huge, aren't they?" Josie said, nodding in the direction of the course. "Is Katrina really going to start with them at that height?"

"I think so." Jill looked worried. "I've always thought it was better to start with them lower and gradually increase them. That's what Sally says you should do."

Josie nodded. It was what her mom had always taught her to do, too.

Just then Katrina came over. Josie and Jill stopped talking and focused on their horses. Watching Katrina tacking Flight up, Josie wondered whether she should say something. She didn't want to look as though she were interfering, but she was convinced Katrina shouldn't start without warming up over some smaller fences first.

"You ready to see how well he really jumps?" Katrina grinned as she mounted.

Josie couldn't stop herself. "Are you sure you shouldn't put the jumps a little lower to start off with?" she blurted out.

Katrina frowned. "Lower?" She looked at the jumps. "No, that height is perfectly fine for Flight. I told you—he can jump three-six easily."

"But my trainer always says you should start with smaller fences and gradually increase the height," Jill said, backing Josie up.

Katrina smiled. "Look, Jill. Don't take this the wrong way, but Flight isn't a school horse. He's a show jumper. These jumps are fine for him." She clicked her tongue. "Come on, boy."

As she rode off, Josie glanced at Jill. Her cheeks were red. Josie felt a surge of anger. She climbed up to sit on the top bar of the fence.

Jill came over to join her, but as she pulled herself onto the fence, she winced, and her hand went to her hip.

"How are you feeling?" Josie asked, in concern.

"I'm fine," said Jill. "My hip's just a little stiff from yesterday. It was all that galloping, I think."

They watched Katrina canter in a circle. Flight saw the jumps and yanked at the reins. When Katrina held him back, he threw his head up and kicked out.

"He looks really excited," said Jill. "It's going to take ages for Katrina to calm him down."

"Here we go!" Katrina called, grinning at them over her shoulder. She turned Flight toward the first jump.

"She can't be jumping him already," Josie said in alarm. "She hasn't even warmed him up yet!"

Flight's ears shot forward, and he raced toward the jump. With a flick of his tail he cleared it easily. As he landed, he grabbed the bit in his teeth and galloped off. Josie could see Katrina sawing on the reins, trying to get him under control. Throwing his head back, he slowed slightly.

"Told you he could do it!" Katrina said, laughing.

"Katrina!" Josie called out. "You really should work him. . . ." Her voice trailed off.

But Katrina wasn't listening. "Still think they're too big for him?" she cut in, smiling.

"No, but . . ."

"Watch this!" Katrina grinned, swinging Flight toward the second jump. Flight pulled hard, his canter increasing to a gallop.

"He's going way too fast!" Jill gasped, grabbing Josie's arm. "He'll never clear it." As she spoke, the same realization seemed to enter Katrina's mind. A look of alarm crossed her face. She pulled on the reins to steady Flight. He tossed his head in irritation, which threw off his balance. Suddenly, the jump was two strides in front of them. Flight gathered himself.

"No!" Josie exclaimed, realizing that he was going to try to jump it.

The chestnut horse launched himself bravely into the air, but he had taken off too late, and the top pole caught his front legs. For a moment Flight seemed to paddle in the air, his front legs desperately reaching out, and then he was falling. He landed heavily on his knees in a clatter of poles.

"Katrina!" Jill cried as her cousin was thrown from the saddle and to the ground.

CHAPTER
FIVE

Flight scrambled up, shook himself, and then looked around with a confused expression. Josie raced across the grass, her heart pounding. She could hear Jill running behind her, her stiff leg slowing her down.

"Katrina!" Josie gasped as she reached the fallen girl. To her relief, Katrina slowly sat up.

"Are you all right?" Josie cried.

"Yes." Katrina gingerly felt her back. "I'm fine. I think I bruised my back a bit, but that's all."

"I should go get my mom," Jill said.

"No, I'm fine," Katrina said. "Don't get her."

Josie helped her to her feet.

"If you say so," Josie said, helping Katrina dust herself off.

"I was so scared!" Jill gasped. "I thought . . ."

"I'm really fine," Katrina insisted, color starting to come back into her face. She looked around for Flight. He had moved off and started to graze. The reins were over his head and one of the stirrup leathers had come off the saddle, but there were no obvious cuts or scrapes on him.

"Here, boy," Katrina said, holding out her hand and walking over.

Flight sidestepped away as if he were going to trot off, but Katrina was too quick for him. She grabbed the dangling reins. Flight snorted, and pranced a little at the end of the reins.

"How is he?" Josie asked anxiously.

Katrina looked him over and carefully ran her hand down his legs. "He's got a few little scratches, but they're not that bad," she said at last. "Would one of you trot him up and down for me, so I can check to see if he's lame?"

"Sure," said Josie, taking the reins.

She clicked her tongue and trotted Flight away

from Katrina. He seemed to move soundly, and when Josie trotted him back to Katrina, she could see that the other girl looked relieved.

"He doesn't look off," Katrina said as Josie halted him. "He's fine."

"Oh, Flight," said Jill, walking over and stroking him. "You are one lucky horse." She looked at Katrina. "I'm so glad he's all right—and that you are. For a minute I thought you had really hurt yourself."

Katrina shrugged. "It was just a fall."

"Yeah, but it looked really bad and—"

"It's no big deal, Jill," Katrina interrupted. She took hold of Flight's reins and put her foot in the stirrup.

"You're not getting on again, are you?" Jill said.

"Of course I am," Katrina said.

She swung herself up. As she landed in the saddle, Flight jumped sideways. "Stand still!" Katrina snapped, kicking the horse. Flight shook his head excitedly. "I said, 'Stand'!" Katrina ordered. She jerked angrily back on the reins, and Flight half reared.

"Maybe you should just take him and let him calm

down in the woods," Josie suggested uncomfortably.

Katrina ignored her and turned Flight away. He tossed his head up and down and started to trot. "Walk!" Katrina said, yanking him in the mouth. Flight plunged sideways, trying to avoid Katrina's swinging legs. "Walk!" she shouted, hitting him again.

Flight skittered under her, his hooves slipping on the grass. Josie crossed her arms tightly across her chest. She hated seeing the horse looking so upset.

Josie stepped forward, but before she could say anything, Katrina looked over her shoulder and called out, "Will you put the jump back up?"

"You're not going to jump him right now, are you?" Jill asked in alarm.

"Of course I am," Katrina said through gritted teeth.

"But you just fell off and—"

"Quit worrying, Jill!" Katrina interrupted angrily. "Now, are you going to put the jump up, or do I have to get off and do it myself?"

Josie and Jill glanced at each other and then silently went over to the fence.

"Let's just put it up as a cross-rail," Josie said in a low voice to Jill. "Flight's going to need a few little jumps to get his confidence back."

Jill nodded. But Katrina frowned when she saw the smaller fence. "What are you doing? I want it the same height as it was before."

Josie finally lost her temper. "That's just being stupid, Katrina! You had a bad fall!" Seeing Katrina's angry expression, she struggled to control her own anger. "I mean, isn't it better to jump him over something low first, and let him get his confidence back?" she added, trying to be more tactful.

"Josie's right, Katrina," Jill added. "You shouldn't jump him really high after a fall like that."

Katrina glared at them. "Are you trying to tell me I don't know what's best for my own horse?"

"No . . . I . . ."

"He *can* jump that height," Katrina insisted. "Now will you please stop being my trainers and put it back up?"

Josie didn't move. Flight might be Katrina's horse, but Josie wasn't going to do something she felt was wrong. Standing right in front of the jump, she shook her head.

"Fine. If you won't put that one up, I'll jump one of the others," Katrina said crossly.

"Katrina . . ." Josie started to protest, but Katrina ignored her. She cantered Flight in a circle and turned him toward another one of the jumps.

He galloped straight at it. Katrina kicked, but at the last minute, a few strides away, she seemed to lose her nerve. Tensing in the saddle, she pulled back on Flight's sensitive mouth. Flight reacted instantly. Throwing up his head, he skidded to a halt, his chest and shoulders crashing into the jump and sending the poles flying. Katrina was thrown forward onto his neck.

Jill gasped in alarm.

As Katrina pushed herself back into the saddle, Josie could see that her face was white and that she seemed to be shaking.

"Katrina, please stop!" Jill cried. "Or at least, take Josie's advice and try a smaller jump."

Josie nodded. "Flight's never going to jump if you're nervous. Leave it till tomorrow."

To Josie's relief, Katrina nodded. "Maybe . . . I . . . I'll just take him up the road to cool off."

She rode toward the gate. Jill hurried over to open it for her. As Katrina rode onto the road, Flight snorted and jogged. "Just walk!" Katrina ordered loudly. But Flight took no notice. Seeing a plastic bag caught in the hedge, he shied violently and shot to the other side of the road.

Josie glanced at Jill. Her face was pale, anxious, and filled with concern.

Meanwhile, Katrina continued to give Flight mixed messages. She kicked him but then pulled on his mouth at the same time. The horse hunched his back as if he were about to buck.

It seemed to be the last straw for Katrina. Turning him around, she let him jog back to the gate. "He's too wound up," she said. "I'm just going to leave him for today." She took her feet out of the stirrups and dismounted.

"Here," Josie said, taking Flight's reins to try to steady him. "Hush, boy." The horse bumped his nose against her shoulder. His neck and shoulders were sweaty, and Josie could feel him shaking.

"Do you want any help cooling him down?" Jill asked, as Katrina ran the stirrups up and yanked the saddle off.

"I'll just stick his sweat sheet on," Katrina muttered.

"Why don't we wash him down for you," Jill said quickly. "We don't mind, do we, Josie?"

Josie shook her head. "No, not at all." It was better than leaving the horse unattended.

"Thanks," Katrina said. "My back's hurting. I'm going to head inside." Carrying the saddle and bridle, she walked quickly back to the house.

Jill fetched Flight's halter and a bucket of water from the hose. As they washed the chestnut horse, he slowly seemed to calm down.

"Have you got any antibiotic cream?" Josie asked Jill as they put on his sweat sheet. "We should put some on his cuts. They're not deep, but if they get infected they could cause a problem."

"It's in the house," said Jill. "I'll get it."

She hurried into the house, leaving Josie alone with Flight. "You silly thing," Josie said, rubbing his neck in small circles. "You really did get yourself in a state." He turned his head and, to her surprise, nuzzled her.

"Do you like this?" she said. The horse snorted.

"I guess you're not used to it," Josie said. She continued to stroke Flight, making little circles with her fingers all along his neck and down his shoulder.

By the time Jill came back with the cream, Flight was standing quietly with his head low and his eyes half closed.

"He looks so calm," Jill said in astonishment.

"I've been stroking him," Josie explained. "He seems to like it." She frowned, still feeling angry with Katrina. "Maybe if Katrina spent more time with him, he wouldn't be so tense all the time!"

Jill bit her lip. "I . . . I guess Katrina really doesn't give him that much attention," she admitted.

Josie could tell Jill didn't want to be disloyal to her cousin, so she dropped the subject and focused on cleaning up Flight's cuts.

When they had put the cream on all of Flight's scrapes and turned him out into the field, Jill said, "Should we go find Katrina to make sure she's all right?"

Josie nodded. Her temper had simmered down, and she was starting to feel sorry for Katrina. It had been a horrible fall, and Katrina was probably feeling really bad about what had happened.

"First I want to check on Faith," Jill said. Josie knew that her friend wanted to make sure her own horse was safe and happy. Faith whinnied a friendly greeting when Jill got to her stall.

"Good girl," Jill said as she gently stroked Faith's nose.

Being with Faith made Josie feel better, too.

They left the barn and went into the house. Music was coming from Katrina's bedroom. Josie hesitated and then knocked on the door.

"Yeah?" Katrina called out above the music.

"It's us," said Josie. "Can we come in?"

"Of course," said Katrina, opening the door. To Josie's surprise, she looked quite cheerful. She had changed out of her riding clothes and was wearing khaki shorts and a red halter top. She had a hairbrush in her hand.

"Are . . . are you all right?" Jill asked.

Katrina laughed brightly. "Of course—why wouldn't I be?"

Jill looked quickly at Josie. "Well, it's just that you looked kind of upset before and . . ."

"Me? I'm not upset," Katrina said. "It was only a little fall. Flight will be fine tomorrow. So," she said, quickly changing the subject, "what time are we going swimming?"

With everything that had happened, Josie had almost forgotten that they were supposed to go swimming with Anna. "Um, two o'clock," she replied. "But if you don't want to go after everything that's—"

"I want to go," Katrina interrupted. "Is there a diving board at this pool?"

Josie nodded.

"Great! Just wait till you see me do a somersault dive into the water." Katrina looked them up and down. "Are you two going to get changed?"

"Er . . . yes," Josie stammered. She felt totally taken aback. She had been expecting to find Katrina quiet and unhappy. Instead, she was as bubbly as always and acting as if the fall had never happened.

"Well, get going," said Katrina. "When you're ready we can have some lunch. I'm starving!"

Barnston Hall was a huge, stone mansion that had been turned into a school. During the school year, the swimming pool was just for the students to use, but in the summer, local people could buy season passes and come to swim whenever they wanted.

Anna's mom pulled into the parking lot, and they all got their towels and bags out of the trunk.

"Well, I'm sure you don't want me hanging around," Mrs. Marshall said to them as they walked down the path to the swimming pool. "I'll be over at the quiet end by the oak trees if you want me."

"Thanks, Mom," smiled Anna. "See you later."

The three girls stood for a moment and looked around, checking out the best spots.

"Let's go over by the diving board," Anna suggested.

Josie and the others nodded and went to find four chairs. They put down their bags and laid out their towels. It had turned into a really hot afternoon, and the water looked inviting.

"Are you okay to swim?" Katrina asked Jill as they took off their shorts and tops. "I mean, with your hip and everything."

"Yup, actually swimming's really good exercise for me," Jill said. "The therapist said I should do it instead of horseback riding." She grinned. "But I had other ideas!" She pulled out some sunscreen. "Anybody need some?"

"Me, definitely!" said Josie. Her pale skin would burn after only a few minutes in the sun.

They quickly rubbed on some lotion. Katrina was the first to finish. She ran to the edge of the pool and dived in.

"What are you waiting for?" she called out as she surfaced. "It's great in here!"

Anna jumped in after her, and Josie and Jill followed. The water was wonderfully cool, and they chased each other up and down playing catch and trying to do handstands in the shallow end.

After a while Josie pulled herself up onto the side to watch the other swimmers. The sun warmed her shoulders, and she sighed happily.

"You'll burn if you sit there too long," Anna said.

"I know," Josie sighed. "But I can do it for a few minutes." She looked enviously at Anna's olive skin. "It's not fair. You're getting tan already."

"I'm going to dive," Katrina said, swimming over with Jill. "Anyone want to join me?"

"Nah, I'm going to sit here for a bit," Josie said, and Anna nodded in agreement.

"I'll go and get us some ice cream," said Jill. "What kind does everyone want?"

"Black cherry, please," said Anna.

"Strawberry for me," said Josie.

"Chocolate, please," Katrina said. She dove underwater and swam over to the deep end.

"So, how was this morning?" Anna asked Josie when they were alone.

Josie told her all about Katrina's fall.

Anna looked shocked. "Is Flight okay?"

"Yes—luckily," Josie said. "I should have tried harder to stop her. Flight was obviously not ready."

"It's not your fault," Anna protested. "She shouldn't have tried to jump so high, so soon."

"Watch this!" Katrina called to them. She ran to the end of the diving board and somersaulted cleanly into the water. She surfaced and swam back toward the ladder.

"Bet I can flip twice this time," Katrina called to them, laughing.

"So, what do you think of her?" Josie asked Anna in a low voice.

"She seems fun, but she shows off a lot," Anna muttered.

Josie thought about the way Katrina had ridden that morning. "I guess she does," Josie admitted, as

Katrina plunged into the water. "I mean, she didn't need to jump so high today. It was just like she wanted to prove how cool she was."

Anna frowned. "Are you going to say something to her? If she's hurting Flight just to impress people, then someone should tell her how ridiculous that is."

Just then, Josie saw Jill coming toward them, three ice-cream cones in her hands. "No," she said quickly. "It would upset Jill. She thinks Katrina's amazing. Please don't say anything, Anna."

Anna sighed. "My lips are sealed." She saw Josie's doubtful look. "Really. They are shut tight," she insisted.

Josie looked at her gratefully, and then her eyes wandered to the pool.

Anna followed her gaze. "I wonder how Flight will be tomorrow. It sounds like he got pretty spooked," she said.

Josie nodded. Tomorrow was going to be very interesting.

CHAPTER SIX

Josie was still wondering what to do about Flight and Katrina the next morning as she and her mother did errands. "Mom, what would you do if a horse was really excitable?" Josie asked as they walked across the parking lot of Harker's, the local tack shop and feed store.

Her mom considered the question for a moment. "Well, first I'd check to see what he was getting fed—too much food can make a horse excitable. If the feed portion was correct for his build and his workload, then I'd spend lots of time working him slowly to calm him down. Why do you ask? Is Charity giving you trouble?"

"Oh, no. No, it's Flight," Josie explained as she pushed open the door and breathed in the welcoming smell of grains, oats, and new leather. "He seems really tense. I don't think it's the feed—he just gets a normal mix, like Faith. But Katrina does gallop and jump him a lot, sometimes without even warming him up."

"That won't help if he's the excitable type," Mrs. Grace said. They went over to the counter and waited for the customer before them to be served. "And I'm sure that being in a new environment might be making him tenser than usual. High-strung horses don't always take well to changes in their surroundings." She looked thoughtful. "Maybe Katrina could try giving him an herbal or mineral supplement to help him adjust. There are quite a few that claim to calm horses down."

The customer in front of them took her change and left. Mrs. Grace turned from Josie to greet the middle-aged man behind the counter. "Hello, Frank," she smiled. "Can we have a bag of the usual feed, please?"

"Sure thing," he replied. As he punched some buttons on the cash register, he frowned. "I didn't mean to eavesdrop, but did I just hear you talking about supplements?"

"A friend of Josie's has a very excitable horse," Mrs. Grace said.

"Well, I might have just the thing to help," Frank said. "It's a new herbal mix called Calm Down." He rifled among the papers around the register and handed them a leaflet. "It's completely natural, based on honey and a plant called valerian, and it's fully approved for use with competition horses and ponies. I'm getting some free samples in a few days—your friend's welcome to try some if she likes," he said to Josie.

Josie looked at her mom. "What do you think?"

"It might be a good idea," said Mrs. Grace, flicking through the leaflet. "If Flight is feeling unsettled, then this could be just what he needs to take the edge off his excitement. But it shouldn't be the full-time solution. Katrina needs to work through this with Flight. Why don't you show her the leaflet and see what she has to say?"

"I'll give you a call when the samples come in," Frank offered.

"Thanks, Frank." Josie wondered what Katrina would say. She had arranged to ride to Jill's that afternoon. She'd ask Katrina then, she decided.

When Josie arrived at Jill's house there was no sign of Jill or Katrina. Josie untacked Charity, put her in the field with the other horses, and then went up to the house.

She found the girls in the kitchen with Mrs. Atterbury.

"Hello, Josie." Mrs. Atterbury greeted her.

"Mom made cookies," Jill said.

"Help yourself," said Mrs. Atterbury, nodding toward a plate of cookies on the counter.

Josie took one and sat down. It was still warm from the oven.

"They're delicious, aren't they?" said Katrina, helping herself to another.

"Mmmm," said Josie through a mouthful of cookie. "You're a great baker, Mrs. Atterbury."

"Thank you," Mrs. Atterbury smiled. She went over to the sink. "Are you all going for a ride this afternoon?"

Jill nodded. "I guess we should go and get the

horses." She stood up. "Thanks for the cookies, Mom."

"My pleasure. You three have fun."

"We will," Josie promised, following Jill to the door. "Are you coming, Katrina?" she asked. Katrina was still sitting at the table.

Katrina hesitated and then stood up. "Of course I am."

As they walked down the sunny yard toward the field, Josie remembered her news. "Mom and I were in the tack shop this morning and the clerk was telling us about this new herbal supplement. It's good for calming down horses." She told Katrina all about it. "He said you can try a free sample," she finished, looking at Katrina to see her reaction.

"I guess there's no harm in trying it." Katrina shrugged. "But it probably won't work."

"It might, though," Jill said hopefully.

"And think about it, if Flight is calmer, then he's less likely to make mistakes when he's jumping," Josie put in. "You said he sometimes gets so excited that he knocks the jumps down," she added as they walked up to the field gate.

Katrina didn't say anything. Her eyes were fixed

on Flight, who was playing with Faith. Putting his head down, he bucked.

"Wouldn't it be great if it worked?" Josie pressed. "At least it would give you a chance to work through things."

"I said I'll try it!" Katrina snapped. "Can you stop talking about it?"

Josie recoiled in shock. She'd only been trying to help. For a moment none of them spoke. Katrina's brusque words hung in the air among them.

Katrina shut her eyes and took a breath. "I'm sorry," she said, sighing. "I didn't mean to snap at you."

"No problem," said Josie, feeling confused.

There was a pause. "Should . . . should I get the halters?" Jill asked timidly.

Katrina hesitated and then said, "Actually, don't bother with Flight's. He looks a bit stiff. I think I'll just give him the day off."

Jill looked surprised. "He doesn't look stiff," she said, watching as Flight walked briskly across the grass.

"I think he does," Katrina insisted. She cleared her throat. "Look, you two go on without me. I'll

. . . I'll see you later." She turned and hurried back to the house.

Josie and Jill stared after her.

"What's going on with her?" Josie asked Jill in astonishment.

"I have no idea," Jill replied. "She's in a really bad mood all of a sudden."

"Well, Flight doesn't look stiff to me," Josie said, studying the chestnut horse as he played in the field.

Jill shrugged. "Oh, well, let's go catch Faith and Charity."

Josie followed Jill and fetched two halters.

Soon Faith and Charity were groomed and tacked up. As the girls walked down the road, Flight trotted over to the fence and whinnied. He was moving as smoothly as ever.

"He looks fine," said Jill. "Why did Katrina insist on saying he was off?"

"I don't know." Josie thought about the weird mood Katrina had been in. "You don't think it was an excuse not to ride, do you?" she asked slowly.

"An excuse?" Jill frowned. "Why would Katrina make an excuse *not* to ride?"

Josie hesitated. She didn't know how much she

could say to Jill. "Maybe her fall yesterday scared her," she suggested.

"Scared?" Jill laughed in astonishment. "But she's the bravest person I know. Nothing scares her."

"But it *was* a pretty nasty spill," Josie pointed out. "It would have frightened the best rider."

"She didn't seem fazed," Jill said. "You saw her trying to do that jump again." She shook her head. "Katrina's not scared. No way."

So why did she say Flight was stiff? Josie thought. She didn't want to push Jill. "Come on," she said, changing the subject. "Let's trot."

Josie and Jill had a great time by the river. They rode the horses through the shallow water and then let them graze for a while under the shade of the trees.

When they got back to Jill's house after their ride, the girls turned Faith and Charity out to graze and went to find Katrina. They found her sunbathing in the backyard.

"How was your ride?" she asked, sitting up as they came around the side of the house. "It was a great day for it." Seeing Katrina's smiling face,

Josie felt a flicker of doubt about her earlier suspicions.

"It was great out there," Jill told Katrina. "You should have come."

"Yeah, I wish Flight hadn't been so stiff."

"We could go again tomorrow," Josie suggested.

"Maybe," Katrina shrugged. "I'll have to see how Flight is doing." She changed the subject. "So, what are you two going to do now?"

"We thought we might sit outside and clean our tack," Jill answered. "Do you want to join us?"

Katrina stretched lazily. "No, I think I'll stay here. Feel free to do mine if you want."

Josie couldn't believe Katrina could be so lazy, but she was even more shocked by Jill's response.

"All right," said Jill. "I like cleaning tack. Come on, Josie, let's get some water."

They got the water and two pails and sat down by the field with their bridles, saddles, and girths.

"It's weird how Katrina doesn't do things like clean tack or groom," remarked Jill.

"It's silly! I love anything to do with horses, even

if it is hard work. That's the whole point of riding horses." Josie rolled the bottoms of her jodhpurs up to her knees.

Jill threw a sponge into the bucket. Water splashed onto Josie's bare legs.

"Watch it!" Josie exclaimed. "You're drenching me, here!"

Jill laughed. "Sorry! You looked like you needed cooling down!"

Josie chucked her sponge at her. "Oh, yeah, well, I'm not the only one!" The sponge hit Jill's shoulder, leaving a wet splotch on Jill's blue T-shirt.

Jill grabbed another sponge. Josie ducked, but it was too late. The sponge landed with a soggy thud against her ear.

"Yuck!" she cried. Picking up the sponge, she threw it at Jill. Within a minute, the battle was in full swing. The horses looked on curiously as wet sponges flew back and forth through the air.

Soon the bucket was empty, and the tack was still dirty. The area around the gate was soaking, and the four sponges lay scattered on the grass.

Jill pushed her wet hair out of her face. "I'm drenched!" she laughed.

"Me, too." Josie grinned. "Who ever said cleaning tack was boring?"

"Josie!" Mrs. Grace knocked on Josie's bedroom door. It was a few days later, and Josie was lying on her bed, reading. "Frank Harker just called," she said when Josie opened the door. "The samples of that herbal supplement came in. If you want, we can go get one and take it over to Jill's."

"Sure," Josie said eagerly. "I'll give Jill a call to make sure she'll be there." She went downstairs and picked up the phone.

Jill answered after a few rings.

"The man from the tack shop just called," Josie told her. "That Calm Down stuff just arrived. Mom said we could go pick it up and bring it over now."

"Actually, I'm on my way out the door," said Jill. "I've got an appointment with the hip specialist."

"Oh," Josie said, feeling disappointed.

"But Katrina will be here, and it's for her, anyway," Jill went on. Her voice dropped. "To be honest, I'm kind of worried about Flight. He keeps pacing by the fence, and he looks agitated. Katrina says he's still stiff, but he looks fine to me."

"Well, I'll come by with the supplement and take a look," Josie said.

She put the phone down and frowned. So Katrina still hadn't ridden Flight. Why? Josie thought back to the day of the fall. Katrina had gotten back on him, but she had seemed shaken up. Josie could remember her pulling on Flight's mouth and shouting at him. And then, when he had stopped at the fence, she had looked really annoyed.

"Honey . . ." said her mom, seeing Josie's expression. "Are you all right?"

"No," Josie admitted.

"What's the matter?"

"Katrina keeps saying that Flight is stiff and that she can't ride him." Josie hesitated. "But I think it might be an excuse. I think the fall she had the other day might have scared her more than she's willing to admit. I wouldn't care that much, but I think she's neglecting Flight."

"Really?" said her mom.

Josie nodded.

Mrs. Grace thought for a moment. "How about I take a look at Flight when we drop the supplement off at Jill's? I don't want to interfere with someone else's horse, but if Flight *is* stiff, then he should be seen by a vet, and if he isn't—and you're right about Katrina—then the sooner she faces up to the fact that she's just making excuses not to ride him, the better. Maybe if she hears it from someone new, she'll get back on."

Josie looked at her in relief. "Thanks, Mom. That would be great."

When Josie and Mrs. Grace arrived at the Atterburys' house, Flight was pacing up and down the fence just as Jill had described.

"He's a gorgeous horse," Mrs. Grace commented. "But Jill was right; he does look tense."

Just then, Katrina came out of the house. "Hello," she said. "Jill said you were coming."

"Hello, Katrina," Mrs. Grace smiled. "I'm Josie's mom. We've brought you the supplement from the tack shop."

"Thank you," said Katrina, taking it. "Do I owe you any money?"

"No, it's a free sample." Josie's mom glanced around. "How is Flight doing? Josie mentioned that you had a hard time the other day. Have you had a chance to ride him since then?"

"He's been kind of stiff," Katrina said quickly.

Mary Grace frowned. "That's a little worrisome. Any stiffness from the fall should have worn off by now. I can take a look at him, if you want. I'm sure Josie mentioned that I used to run a stable. I've had horses for years, and I know that sometimes it helps to have a second opinion. And if he is still stiff, it might mean there's a more serious problem."

Katrina hesitated. "Okay," she said at last. "I'll go and catch him."

She got Flight's halter and went into the field. Flight walked up to her, pushing his nose eagerly forward. As she buckled up the strap, he nudged her with his muzzle. Katrina led him back toward the fence.

"Just trot him up and down the road for me," said Mrs. Grace.

Katrina clicked her tongue and tugged harshly on the lead rope. He plunged forward. "Whoa!" she snapped, yanking the lead.

The chestnut horse slowed down. Finally, Katrina dragged him to a halt beside Mrs. Grace.

"Well, he looks just fine," said Josie's mom. She began to examine his legs, neck, and back, feeling the muscles with skilled hands.

When she was finished, she stopped and smiled at Katrina. "I can't find any soreness. But just to be sure, why don't you tack him up so I can see what he's like under saddle?"

A trapped look appeared on Katrina's face. "I . . . I . . ." Suddenly she put her hand to her back. "Actually, Mrs. Grace, my back's been hurting since the fall. I don't think I should ride just yet."

Mrs. Grace raised her eyebrows. "But the fall was several days ago. If your back's still hurting, you should see a doctor."

"It's not that bad," Katrina said hastily. "I think I just need to rest it."

Josie remembered how good Katrina's diving had been at the pool the day after the fall. If her back had really been hurting she wouldn't have been able to do that. Having a sore back seemed like just another excuse. She felt a wave of sympathy for Katrina. She seemed really scared to ride Flight.

"I'll just put him back in the field," Katrina said.

"Whatever you want to do, Katrina," said Mrs.

Grace. "I hope your back gets better soon. High-strung horses like Flight usually need a lot of exercise and attention. If you don't feel like riding him, maybe you could lunge him. That way, he gets out, but all you have to do is stand in the middle of the circle and make sure he keeps moving around the lunge line."

"I'll see how I'm feeling tomorrow," said Katrina, avoiding Mrs. Grace's eyes.

Mrs. Grace looked around. "Well, come on, Josie. We should probably go."

Katrina waved good-bye.

"Well?" Josie said to her mom as they drove away.

"It looks like you're right," she said. "Katrina does seem to be making up plenty of excuses not to ride." She frowned. "You say she was a confident rider before the fall?"

"Yes, she couldn't have been more confident. She was almost too confident," Josie replied. "It's just so strange. How could one fall have made her this frightened, Mom?"

"It's not unusual," Mrs. Grace answered. "The more confident a rider is, the more severely a bad fall can affect them. It's as if, until then, they felt invincible, and the realization that they—or the horse—might get injured shakes them. Still," she added, seeing Josie's worried expression, "it's usually just a phase. I would think that once Katrina conquers her initial fear and starts riding again, her confidence will come back quickly."

"But when?" Josie asked.

"I honestly don't know," Mrs. Grace admitted. "But the sooner the better, because the longer she puts it off the harder it will be." She shook her head. "It's a pity Flight isn't calmer. He doesn't appear to be the ideal horse for someone who's feeling a bit nervous."

"No," Josie agreed. She grew silent. She really wanted to help Katrina, but she didn't know how.

Suddenly she had an idea. "Katrina doesn't have to ride Flight right away! She could ride Faith until she gets her confidence back. I'm sure Jill wouldn't mind. I could call her tonight." She nodded, caught up in her plan. "We could try and persuade Katrina tomorrow and—"

"Hang on a minute, Josie," her mom interrupted. Josie looked at her.

"I know you want to help," Mary Grace said gently. "But I think you're going to have to let Katrina deal with this on her own. If you go there tomorrow and try to badger her into riding Faith, I think you might do more harm than good. People with strong personalities, like Katrina, never like admitting their weaknesses. I think you're just going to have to give her time to come to terms with this herself."

"But what if it takes days or even weeks? And what about Flight?" Josie protested. "He really needs to be ridden." She cast around for a solution to the problem. "I guess I could offer to ride him," she suggested.

"No," her mom said quickly. "You can't do that. Knowing Flight needs riding is the best reason for Katrina to get on him again. If you ride him, she doesn't need to, and she won't."

"But he's really unhappy, Mom."

Mrs. Grace sighed. "I know it's difficult, Josie. But I really do think you'll make things worse if you try to interfere."

Josie fell silent. An image of Flight pacing up and down the fence came before her. She didn't think she could bear to see him continuing to look so miserable. "I just want to help."

Her mom glanced across at her. "I know you do, sweetie," she said softly. "But, right now, I don't think there's anything you can do."

CHAPTER SEVEN

Over the next few days, Josie tried hard not to interfere, but it proved difficult. Every time she rode over to Jill's, she saw Jill taking care of Flight. Katrina would come out of the house to talk to Jill and Josie, but the only time she went near Flight was to give him his dinner. Josie thought that Katrina only did that much because she thought Jill's parents would have become suspicious if she never went out to the stable.

"Poor boy," said Josie one afternoon as she tied Flight up. "You don't understand what's going on, do you?" The horse pushed his nose against her hand.

Stroking his tangled mane, Josie frowned. Flight's neck and legs were dusty, and he had rubbed the top of his tail, so that it stood out in spiky clumps. "She could at least groom you," she muttered. "Even if she's too scared to ride, I don't see why she can't brush you. It's too much for Jill to take care of two horses."

Just then, the back door of the house opened, and Katrina and Jill came out.

"Hi," Jill called. "I wasn't expecting you so early. I haven't groomed Faith yet."

"I don't mind waiting," Josie told her. "I'll give you a hand."

Katrina walked over with them, but, although Flight stretched out his nose to her, she didn't touch him. In fact, she hardly even looked at him. "Are you going out for a ride?" she asked as Jill went to catch Faith.

"Yup," Josie answered. "Do you want to come with us?"

"Not today," Katrina said. "My back still hurts." She sat down on an upturned bucket.

Josie wanted to tell her to stop pretending, but, remembering what her mom had said, she bit back the words.

Jill led Faith over and tied her up. Picking

up a soft brush, Josie went to help her groom.

As they brushed Faith, Flight started walking up and down along the fence again. Katrina didn't seem to notice. She was too busy rolling up her sleeves to examine her tanned arms.

Looking at the beautiful horse's unhappy eyes, Josie couldn't contain herself any longer. "Why don't you groom him?" she burst out.

Katrina looked up in surprise. "What?"

"You could groom Flight," Josie repeated, trying to keep the anger out of her voice.

"I'll do it later." Katrina shrugged. She held out her arms and changed the subject. "You know, I'm getting really tan with all this sun."

Josie stared at her. How could she talk about her suntan when Flight was looking so miserable? "Katrina!" she exclaimed, forgetting her mother's warning in her frustration. "Can't you see how unhappy Flight is? Jill can't keep covering for you. Just because you're scared doesn't mean you can stop looking after him!"

"Scared? What are you talking about?"

"You're scared of riding him—it's so obvious!" Josie stated bluntly.

"Josie—" Jill started to say, but then Katrina interrupted her.

"I am *not* scared!" she said, getting to her feet and glaring at Josie.

"Oh, really? So why do you keep making excuses not to ride him?" Josie demanded. "Because they are excuses. Flight's not stiff. Your back doesn't hurt. You're just frightened, Katrina. Admit it!"

"I am *not*!" Katrina insisted, her cheeks flushing. "My back *has* been hurting!"

"No, it hasn't," Josie said fiercely. "You managed to dive and swim just fine the other day, and if it was still hurting, you'd have gone to the doctor by now. You just don't want to ride!"

"That's *so* not true!" Katrina cried.

Grabbing Flight's bridle she marched to the gate. "You think I'm scared? Then let's go out for a ride. We'll see who's scared then, Josie Grace."

Josie frowned. This wasn't the way she had wanted to get Katrina riding again. Her temper subsided as quickly as it had flared up. "Katrina," she said. "You don't have to take Flight out—"

"Frightened you're not going to be able to keep up with me?" Katrina taunted.

"No," Josie replied. "But—"

"If you're coming, come," Katrina snapped, pulling off Flight's sheet. "If not, I'll go on my own." She stomped over to the tack room.

Jill looked anxiously at Josie. "Why did you say that to her? She's so upset."

"I know," Josie said. "I didn't mean to. But it's true, Jill."

"I guess she *might* have been making excuses," Jill admitted. "So what are we going to do? Are we going to ride with her?"

"I think we'd better," said Josie. Flight hadn't been ridden for almost a week, and Katrina wasn't thinking properly. They couldn't let her take him out on her own. He might throw her off.

Katrina marched back with the saddle and bridle. Without saying a word to them, she threw the tack onto Flight's back. Josie and Jill quickly saddled Faith.

Katrina mounted, her jaw set in a furious line, and kicked Flight on down the drive.

"I've never seen her this angry," Jill said, as Josie gave her a quick leg up.

"I guess the only thing we can do is stay with her

and try to make sure nothing bad happens," Josie said, hastily mounting Charity.

They set off at a trot down the drive. Charity fought for her head, wanting to catch up with Flight. "Easy, girl," Josie soothed, sitting deep in the saddle.

Charity snorted impatiently, but she slowed down and started to listen to Josie's signals.

At the entrance to the woods, Josie and Jill caught up with Katrina.

Flight saw the sandy track and started to plunge forward with excitement. His chestnut neck was already lathered with sweat. As he moved forward, Katrina stiffened in alarm, her hands grabbing at the reins. Seeing Josie, she gritted her teeth and leaned forward in the saddle. "Come on, boy!" she said, nudging her heels against Flight's sides.

"Katrina!" Jill exclaimed. "Wait! We don't have to go so fast!"

Katrina ignored her. She urged Flight on to a gallop. Jill and Josie raced after her. Josie felt her heart thumping in her chest. As she struggled to keep up with Katrina, she wished that she had followed her mom's advice. What if Flight—or Katrina—got hurt? It would all be her fault!

When they reached a fork in the path, Katrina pulled up. Her eyes glittered recklessly.

"Let's go home, Katrina," said Josie as Charity halted. "Look, I'm sorry I said you were scared."

"I'm not going home!" Katrina exclaimed, her voice high. "I'm having fun!" But she didn't look as if she were. Then she added snidely, "Aren't you?"

"Katrina—" Josie began again.

"I'm going to the river," Katrina interrupted. She trotted Flight down the fork that led to the road.

Josie and Jill exchanged worried glances. There didn't seem to be much else they could do, so they followed her.

They clattered along the road at a fast trot until they came to the path that led back into the woods again. Josie patted Charity's neck. She was sweating as much as Flight was.

"Whoa, girl," Josie said soothingly as Charity sidestepped excitedly near the edge of the steep drop. A rock kicked loose by Charity's hooves bounced down the dry, sandy bank and landed in the bushes below.

"Scared?" Katrina asked mockingly.

"No, but I don't want her to fall down a steep

bank like that," Josie replied sharply, digging her left heel into Charity's side so that the horse kept well over to the right.

"It's not that big a drop," said Katrina, her eyes narrowing. She rode Flight over to the edge and peered over it. "Bet I could ride down it!"

"Katrina, no!" Jill gasped.

"Why not? Do you think I'm too scared?" Katrina demanded, looking back over her shoulder at them, her eyes full of challenge.

"Don't be stupid, Katrina!" Josie exclaimed, as Flight pranced excitedly, his hooves dislodging several stones that tumbled down the slope. "It's way too steep!"

"Wanna bet?" Gripping tightly on the reins, Katrina kicked Flight forward.

"No!" Jill gasped.

Josie watched in horror as Flight leaped down the bank. He cantered two strides, his head high and his hocks underneath him, and then his back hooves slipped on the sand. Feeling him lose his footing, Katrina grabbed at the reins, pulling harshly on the bit. The movement unbalanced Flight and he flung his head back.

Suddenly the horse was scrabbling desperately with his front legs. Attempting to grab onto his mane, Katrina lost her reins. Horse and rider half slipped, half fell down the slope in a cloud of dust and rocks.

"Katrina!" Jill screamed.

To Josie's enormous relief, she saw Flight regain his footing at the bottom and come to a trembling stop. Katrina was clinging to his neck, half out of the saddle, both feet hanging out of the stirrups.

"Are you okay?" Josie called, her heart pounding. Katrina didn't reply.

"Jill, hold Charity!" Josie said, dismounting and throwing the reins to her friend. In the next instant she was slipping and sliding down the slope, the scrubby bushes tearing at her hands and arms as sand rose in a cloud around her.

"Katrina!" she gasped as she reached the bottom. "Are you all right?"

Looking deathly white, Katrina released her grip on Flight's neck and slid to the ground. She was shaking and looked too shocked to speak. But to Josie's relief, she didn't look as if she had hurt herself.

Flight was another matter. As Katrina slid off

him, he sidestepped and came to a halt, holding up his right foreleg. Bright, red blood trickled from a deep cut over his hoof.

Katrina saw the blood and gasped as her hand flew to her mouth. She swayed, and for a horrible moment, Josie thought she was going to faint.

"Katrina!" Josie fought through the bushes toward them. The thorns tore at her jodhpurs, but she hardly noticed.

"His leg," Katrina whispered, staring at Flight's wound. "Look at his poor leg."

Flight pulled backward. The reins slipped from Katrina's fingers.

"Easy, boy, shhh . . ." Josie said, grabbing the reins. The chestnut horse snorted in alarm. Josie rubbed his neck, trying desperately to keep calm. "Come on, now," she said, in as steady a voice as she could muster. "Let's get you out of these bushes."

At first, Flight refused to move. Then Josie pulled gently on his reins, and he stepped forward a few paces until he was standing at the bottom of the bank on a bare patch of sandy ground.

"How badly hurt is he?" Katrina asked, following Josie and Flight out of the bushes.

Josie crouched down. "I think he must have stepped on himself as he fell," she said, looking at the cut that ran along the back of his hoof. With all the dirt, she couldn't tell how deep the cut was.

"What are we going to do?" Katrina asked, looking around in panic at the thicket of bushes surrounding them. "How are we going to get him out of here?"

"I don't know," Josie admitted quietly.

"We're stuck!" Katrina's voice began to rise in alarm. "Seriously, Josie, what are we going to do?"

"What's going on?" Jill called anxiously from the top of the bank. "Is Flight hurt?"

"Yes," Josie called back. "He's cut his heel and he's bleeding. We need to get help." She handed the reins to Katrina and started climbing the slope, her hands searching for tree roots to hang on to. "I'll go on Charity."

"Don't leave, Josie!" Katrina cried.

Her fear seemed to transmit itself to Flight, who snorted and backed up in alarm.

"Whoa!" Katrina let out a gasp. The movement reopened the wound, causing it to bleed again.

"Josie!" she cried desperately. "I don't want to stay down here alone!"

"Jill will come down and wait with you," Josie promised. They had to get help. It would be quicker for her to go on Charity. She could jump over the logs in the trail, rather than going the long way around on the roads.

"I can't," Jill called down, sounding worried. "I can't climb down a slope like that! Not with my hip the way it is."

Josie stopped. She hadn't thought of that. "You'll have to go and get help, then," she said to Jill. She scrambled to the top of the slope and took Charity's reins. The gray horse nuzzled her in confusion. "When you get home, tell your dad to call a vet and come find us."

Jill nodded.

"We need to get help quickly," Josie urged her. "Flight's bleeding and we need to get the wound cleaned. Trot as fast as you can on the roads, and canter the rest of the way."

Jill looked down the track. A tree trunk blocking the path was just visible. She swallowed. "If I jumped that log, I wouldn't have to go back on the roads."

Josie stared at her. "But it's huge!"

"I know." Jill's voice shook. "But if I jumped it, I'd get home much quicker."

Josie was aware of Flight moving restlessly at the bottom of the slope. While she was desperate to get help as fast as possible, she didn't want to force Jill to jump something so big. She shook her head. "No, Jill, don't worry. Just go around. You don't have to impress anyone or prove anything."

"But I'm doing it for Katrina," Jill replied calmly. She took a deep breath and stared at the log. "I'm going to do it," she said in a determined voice. "For Katrina *and* Flight."

"But—" Josie started to protest.

"Josie," Jill interrupted. "I can jump it. I know it."

She sounded so determined that Josie hesitated. "Well, if you're sure . . ."

Jill nodded. "I am." She stroked Faith's neck. "Come on, Faith," she whispered. "We can do this."

Josie watched as Faith obeyed the touch of Jill's heel and sprang forward into a canter. "We'll be back soon," Jill called over her shoulder.

"Good luck!" Josie cried, her heart pounding.

Jill hardly seemed to hear her. Her face set,

she cantered toward the log. It loomed up ahead of her and Faith, branches sticking out in every direction.

For a moment, Josie saw Jill's back stiffen in hesitation in the saddle and Faith's stride start to slow in response. Josie's heart sank. They weren't going to do it. It was too much to ask. . . .

But suddenly, Jill looked back, and Josie saw her frown in determination. She leaned forward. Faith reacted instantly. Her brown ears pricked up, and her stride lengthened. *One, two, three . . .*

Josie held her breath as she watched.

Sitting deep in the saddle, her hands wrapped in the horse's long mane, Jill threw herself forward as Faith took off. There was one moment where they seemed to hang in midair, and then they were landing, safe, on the other side.

With a swish of her tail, Faith disappeared into the woods.

Relief and amazement rushed through Josie. They'd done it! Help was on the way.

CHAPTER EIGHT

Josie slithered back down the bank. Katrina held on to Flight's reins as he tossed his head restlessly.

"Shhh. . . . Please stand still!" she pleaded.

"Here," Josie said, hurrying over. "Let me take him, Katrina." She took the reins and stroked Flight's neck. "It's all right, boy. You'll be fine."

"What are we going to do? The cut's still bleeding," said Katrina. "What if he's cut an artery? Horses can die from losing too much blood if they cut an artery." She swallowed. "It's all my fault. I was so stupid." A tear trickled down her cheek.

"I'll never forgive myself if he is seriously hurt, Josie."

"It will be okay," Josie said, trying to speak reassuringly, although inside she felt on the verge of panic at the thought that Flight might have cut an artery. That really would have been serious. She took a deep breath. "Look, we've got to stay calm, Katrina. If we get upset, it will just upset Flight."

Katrina's eyes met Josie's. She hesitated, and then she took a deep breath. "You're right," she said. "We've got to stay calm." She shook her head. "I'm sorry I'm being so useless, Josie. I just hate the thought that he's injured because of me."

"Try not to think about it," Josie told her. "We've just got to try and help him."

Katrina nodded. "Yes, it's Flight who matters." She stroked his shoulder. "There, boy. You relax," she said, soothingly. "You're going to be fine."

"Jill will be back soon with her dad. They'll have called the vet."

Katrina looked worried. "But it'll take Jill ages to get home."

"It won't. She jumped the fallen tree," Josie told her. As she spoke, she felt a wave of pride—for Jill and for the steady, trustworthy Faith. Jumping that tree trunk had been an amazing thing for both of them to do.

"Really?" said Katrina, her eyes widening. "Jill really jumped it?"

Josie nodded. "She said she was doing it for you and Flight. She was amazing."

Fresh tears sprang to Katrina's eyes. "That was so brave of her." She swallowed hard. "Oh, this is such a stupid mess, and it's all my fault." A sob escaped from her.

Josie tried to find the words to comfort the older girl, but before she could speak, Flight stretched out his nose and nuzzled Katrina's hair.

Katrina looked up at him. "Flight?" she said in surprise.

The horse blew gently on her, his eyes large and confused. Katrina reached out and rubbed his jaw. Flight stepped closer and nudged her again.

For a moment, Katrina hesitated, and then she stroked the swirl of hair in the middle of Flight's forehead. "I can't believe you still love me after everything I've done to you," she said in a choked voice.

Flight snorted softly.

"Oh, poor Flight," Katrina whispered. "If you get better, I promise I'll make this up to you. I won't ever do anything to hurt you ever again. I won't push you or ignore you. I'll just take really good care of you. Just, please, get better! Please!" She kissed him softly on the nose.

Josie watched them with a lump in her throat, wishing she could say something to make Katrina feel better.

Katrina looked at Flight's injured leg. "Do . . . do you think we should bandage the wound somehow? He's still bleeding."

"We haven't got anything to use as a bandage," Josie pointed out.

Katrina thought for a moment. "We could use socks," she said, pulling off her riding boots. "I don't know if it will help, but it's got to be worth a try."

"Definitely," Josie said, starting to take off her boots. "Here, use mine as well."

Katrina made a bandage by tying the socks together, and then she crouched down by Flight's hoof. Very carefully she wound the makeshift bandage around his leg, pulling it firmly, but not making it too tight.

Flight stamped his foot but Katrina spoke to him softly and he quickly settled down.

"There," Katrina said as she finished.

"That was a great idea," Josie said admiringly.

"Thanks." Katrina smiled shakily. "I'm glad you're here with me, Josie. I—I'm sorry I was so mean earlier."

"It doesn't matter," Josie said. She meant it. What had happened wasn't important. The only thing that mattered now was Flight.

They waited for what seemed like ages. Finally, they heard something.

"Katrina! Josie!"

Hearing Mr. Atterbury's voice, Josie jumped to her feet. "We're down here!" she shouted.

Mr. Atterbury looked over the top of the bank.

"Uncle David!" Katrina called in relief.

Mr. Atterbury began to clamber down the bank. "It's all right," he said. "The vet's on his way. The clinic managed to contact him on his cell phone, and he should be here any minute. Jill's waiting for him up by the road." He hurried over. "So where's he hurt?"

"There." Katrina pointed to Flight's injured leg.

"Dad!" Jill's voice came from the top of the slope. "The vet's here!"

Dr. Vaughan, the vet, slid down the slope, bag in hand. Josie knew him well, as he had often visited her mom's old riding stables. He smiled quickly, but his attention was on Flight. "Let's take a look, shall we?"

Josie waited anxiously. Oh, please, she thought, please let Flight be okay.

Dr. Vaughan crouched down, unwrapped the bandage, and began examining Flight's leg.

"Has he cut an artery?" Katrina asked anxiously.

Dr. Vaughan shook his head. "No, there would be much more blood if he had done that." He straightened up. "In fact, I'd say he's been lucky. It's a fairly deep cut, but once it's cleaned up it should heal quickly. I know there's a lot of blood, but that's not unusual for a wound like this. They often look worse than they are."

"So he's going to be all right?" Katrina asked, her voice trembling.

"He's going to be fine," the vet said.

Katrina buried her face in Flight's neck. "Oh, Flight!"

Josie looked up to the top of the slope, where Jill was watching with a worried expression on her face. "He's going to be fine!" Josie called to her.

"Yes!" Jill cried.

Mr. Atterbury put a big, comforting hand on Katrina's shoulder. "So, what do we do now?" he asked Dr. Vaughan.

"I'll bandage him up and give him a shot of painkillers and antibiotics," the vet said. "Then he should be fine to walk home—although not up this bank. We'll need to clear a path so that he can walk up the hill where it's least steep."

"I brought some clippers with me," Mr. Atterbury said. "Jill warned me about the bushes."

"Great," said the vet. "Once we get him home, I'll clean up the wound properly. His leg will need cleaning for the next three or four days, to make sure there's no dirt trapped inside the wound." He looked at Katrina. "He's going to need a lot of care."

"I'll do anything to make him better," Katrina promised.

Dr. Vaughan smiled at her. "Good. He'll need bran mashes instead of his regular feed, to help keep him calm, and you'll need to check the bandage two times a day. If his leg starts to swell or feel hot, then contact me at once."

"How long will it take him to get better?" Josie asked.

"If he heals well and there's no infection, he should be able to do light work in five to seven days and back to full work in about ten days," Dr. Vaughan said. He patted Flight's neck. "Let's get this guy home."

"Are you coming in the car with me, Jill?" Mr. Atterbury asked when they had reached the road.

Jill nodded. "Poor Faith will be wondering what's happening. I just tied her up with all her tack on and left." She smiled. "And she'd been so good. She jumped the tree trunk perfectly."

"I can't believe you jumped it," Katrina said.

"You were really amazing, Jill," Josie said. "You trusted Faith to jump the tree, and she did."

"Faith's wonderful," Jill smiled. "If I hadn't been riding her I'd never have dared to do it. But I just knew I could trust her."

"Now we'd better get back to her," Mr. Atterbury said.

Jill nodded. "I'll get a bran mash ready for Flight," she told Katrina.

"Thanks," Katrina smiled gratefully.

"See you back at your house," Josie called to Jill and her father, as she led Charity after Flight.

For a while the two girls walked in silence. The only sound was the soft swish of the horses' hooves on the sandy path.

Josie looked across at Katrina. Flight was walking close beside her, and she had one hand on his neck. She looked deep in thought. "It's good that Flight's going to get better soon, isn't it?" Josie said to her.

Katrina nodded. "Yes." She bit her lip. "It's still my fault he's injured, though."

"It was an accident," Josie told her.

"That I caused," Katrina pointed out. "I was showing off. I was trying to prove to you that I wasn't scared." She looked down. "But I was, and that's why he fell. If I hadn't panicked as we went down the hill he wouldn't have lost his balance."

Josie glanced sympathetically at her. Riding Flight down the slope had been a silly thing to do, but Katrina was obviously really sorry. "Just try and forget it," she said. "What's done is done."

"But I can't." Katrina looked at Josie. "What if it happens again?"

"What do you mean?"

"What if I panic next time I'm jumping him?" Katrina shook her head. "You were right, Josie. I am scared. I have been ever since I fell off at that jump the other day."

"You'll get your confidence back," Josie said quickly, wanting to reassure her. "It'll just take some time. You need to keep the jumps low until you stop feeling nervous." Then Josie took a deep breath. She didn't know if she should say anything about how Katrina didn't take care of Flight, but she felt she had to say something. "My mother says that owning a horse is hard work, and most of it is out of the saddle."

Katrina looked at Josie. "I know what you mean. I'm spoiled, because at the stables where Flight is kept, the grooms do all the work." Katrina reached up to stroke Flight's nose. "But I've been watching how Jill cares for Faith. She was so great to look after Flight, too."

"Jill loves Faith and Flight," Josie said.

"Yes, but Flight is my responsibility."

Josie smiled. She was glad to hear that Katrina was seeing things clearly.

"I couldn't bear it if I caused Flight to have another accident." Katrina took a deep breath. "I'm not going to jump him again. Ever."

"But you both love jumping!" Josie exclaimed. "You can't give it up, Katrina."

"I can," Katrina replied, stroking Flight's mane. He turned and pushed her affectionately with his nose.

"But if you don't jump, you'll never get your confidence back," Josie protested.

"And if I do jump, I might end up hurting Flight," Katrina said stubbornly.

"But—" Josie began.

"I don't want to talk about it," Katrina cut in. "I've made up my mind." She put her hand on Flight's neck. "We're not going to jump any more, and that's final."

Josie stared at her. She wanted to argue with her, but it was clear from the determined look on Katrina's face that she wasn't going to talk about it any more. They continued the rest of the way in silence.

When they got back to the field, Katrina untacked

Flight and fed him a bran mash that Jill had prepared. While he ate, she rubbed him down. She seemed to be trying to do everything she could to make up for what had happened. When she had finished, she kissed him on the nose and went into the house looking very subdued.

"Do you think she's okay?" Jill said to Josie.

"I don't know," Josie admitted. "I think she's still really shocked by what happened." She told Jill what Katrina had said about taking better care of Flight and not jumping him any more.

"What?" Jill exclaimed. "Why?"

"She's worried that if she jumps him she might panic and hurt him. She told me she's been feeling scared ever since her fall the other day."

"I can't believe it," Jill said, looking shocked. "She always seems so brave." She shook her head. "I'm sure she'll change her mind."

Josie remembered the look on Katrina's face. "I really don't know if she will," she said heavily.

Josie thought about Flight and Katrina all night. As soon as she got up the next morning, she groomed Charity and set off for Jill's.

She arrived to find Flight tied up to the fence and Katrina coming out of the tack room with a grooming kit.

"Hi!" Josie called. "How's Flight?"

"Still hurt," Katrina replied. "But the wound is clean. I flushed it out about an hour ago."

Josie dismounted. "Where's Jill?"

"Up at the house," Katrina said. "Her hip was hurting when she woke up. I think it was all the galloping and jumping yesterday. So Aunt Jane is making her rest." She took the soft brush out of the grooming box and began to brush Flight's tail, gently separating the strands one by one.

"Do you want a hand?" Josie offered.

"No thanks. I want to do it." Katrina straightened up. "I was thinking more about taking care of Flight last night. I ride him and take him to shows, but I never just talk to him and groom him, the way you and Jill do with Charity and Faith. But I should—he's my horse." She patted Flight. "So from now on, things are going to be different. I might not be jumping him, but I'm going to take care of him really well."

Josie frowned. "So I guess you haven't changed your mind about jumping him?"

"No," Katrina said firmly.

"But Katrina, he loves jumping," Josie protested. "You can't just give up on it." As Josie spoke, Faith wandered up to Flight and touched noses with him, her dark eyes wise and knowing. The sight of her nuzzling Flight made Josie remember the idea she'd had a few days ago. "Look, all you need is to get your confidence back. Why don't you jump Faith? She's so good. I'm sure jumping her would help you get over your nerves, and then you'd be fine to jump Flight."

Katrina glanced at Faith. "But what if I pulled on her mouth?" she fretted. "What if I panicked and hurt her?"

"You won't!" Josie said. "Faith's too sensible for that. I think it's worth a try."

"I guess so," Katrina said uncertainly.

"I'm sure Jill won't mind," Josie said. "We can go and ask her."

"I—I don't know," Katrina replied. "I'd never forgive myself if something bad happened to Faith because of me."

"What are you two talking about?"

Jill was coming through the yard. She was limping slightly, but otherwise looked fine.

Josie looked at Katrina. She didn't want to give the other girl's secret away. To her relief, Katrina didn't try to hide what they'd been talking about.

"Josie's trying to persuade me to ask you if I can jump Faith," Katrina admitted.

"Jump Faith?" Jill echoed. "Well, of course you can, but why?"

"Because . . ." Katrina took a deep breath. "Because ever since we had that wipeout the other day, I've been scared of jumping. Josie thinks that maybe if I jump Faith, I'll feel better." The words sounded as if they were hard for her to say. Her cheeks turned red, and she looked at the ground.

Jill immediately looked understanding. "I'm not surprised you felt a little scared," she said. "It *was* an awful fall. I'd have been terrified if it had happened to me."

Katrina smiled gratefully at her.

"I'll go and tack Faith up now for you, if you like," Jill offered.

"And I'll go and put a few jumps up," said Josie.

Katrina stiffened. "I don't know if I want to jump just yet. Maybe in a few days."

"You don't have to jump right away. Just start on the flat," Jill said.

"Yeah," said Josie. "Do what makes you feel comfortable."

Katrina shook her head, looking almost angry with herself. "You both must think I'm so pathetic!"

"Of course we don't!" Jill exclaimed. "After my car accident I was terrified about riding."

Katrina frowned. "Really?"

Jill nodded. "I didn't want to fall off and hurt myself all over again. I was a nervous wreck. But then I got Faith." A smile flickered across her face as she looked at the bay mare. "She was so wonderful, sensible, and calm. She made me feel I could do anything. And I can. Look how we jumped that tree yesterday." Her eyes met Katrina's. "Please give her a chance, Katrina."

Katrina hesitated. "I don't know."

"She helped me so much. Maybe she'll be able to help you, too," Jill said softly.

There was a pause and then, to Josie's relief, Katrina nodded. "I'll try," she said.

CHAPTER
NINE

After putting her own saddle on Faith, Katrina mounted and rode around the field. At first, she looked tense, but as horse and girl worked together, her whole body seemed to relax. Soon, she had Faith trotting and cantering in smooth circles.

"She's got an amazing canter!" Katrina called as she rode past Josie and Jill. "She's so comfortable it feels like you're in a rocking chair!"

"Do you want to try a jump?" Josie called out.

Katrina shook her head.

"Go on," Jill said, encouraging her.

"I'll just go ahead and lower one of them in case you feel like it," Josie said, walking to the closest jump.

As she lowered the ends of the poles into a cross-rail, she watched Katrina do a figure eight on Faith. They looked good together. Josie put the poles down another few holes. The fence looked low and inviting. "There you go!" she called to Katrina. "Why don't you try it? It's just a small one."

Katrina halted and looked at the jump. "What if I do something wrong?"

"Faith won't mind," said Jill. "I promise."

Katrina shook her head. "No. I can't do it."

"You can," Josie told her.

"Just trust Faith," Jill urged. "She'll jump it, Katrina."

As if sensing Katrina's fear, Faith swung her head around and nuzzled her leg.

Katrina stroked her neck. "I'll try."

Josie smiled in delight. "You'll be fine."

Katrina took a deep breath and, touching her heels to Faith's sides, circled in front of the jump.

"Come on, Faith," breathed Josie as Katrina turned

Faith toward the fence. She saw Katrina tense up as Faith picked up the canter, but Faith didn't flicker. The bay mare cantered on and cleared the little fence perfectly.

Katrina broke into a broad grin. "We did it!"

"You looked great," Jill said as Katrina cantered over to the gate.

"It actually felt all right." Katrina patted Faith. "She feels so safe. You're right, Jill. You just know you can trust her."

"Jump her again," Josie urged.

Katrina picked up a canter and took Faith over the fence several times. Each time, she looked more and more confident, and after the fourth time she jumped the fence, she pushed Faith on and cleared the other three jumps in the field, too.

Landing over the final one, she grinned in delight. "Wow! I'd almost forgotten how much I love jumping!" she exclaimed. She rode over, patting Faith. "She's wonderful, Jill!"

"I told you," said Jill.

"She seems to be enjoying it, too!" Josie said, looking at Faith's pricked ears.

"She doesn't normally jump so high," Jill said,

looking at the last fence Katrina had jumped. "I wish I were brave enough to jump as high as that," she added wistfully.

"What are you talking about?" Katrina said in astonishment. "You're very brave."

"No, I'm not," Jill protested.

"You are. You jumped that big log yesterday," Katrina told her.

"But that wasn't brave. I was scared stiff."

"So?" said Josie. "You were scared, but you still did it. That takes real guts."

"Josie's right," Katrina agreed. "It's not brave to do something you're not scared of. You're only brave when you do something even though you feel frightened."

"I just wanted to help you," Jill said, looking embarrassed.

"Well, I think you're one of the bravest people I know," Katrina told her. "Jumping that log, starting to ride again after your accident . . . You're amazing."

Jill blushed. "It's all because of Faith. I couldn't have done either of those things without her."

"She's great. I certainly wouldn't have started

jumping again without her help," Katrina said, patting Faith's neck. "Thank you for letting me ride her, Jill. She's one in a million."

Jill stroked Faith's forelock and smiled. "I know."

Over the next week, Katrina rode Faith every day. She and Jill took turns and Katrina even tried riding sidesaddle. When she wasn't riding Faith, she spent all her time with Flight. She cleaned his leg, made him bran mashes, and groomed him until his coat shone. He began to walk up to the fence whenever she came out of the house.

"He's so much more affectionate with you now," Josie remarked as she watched the handsome chestnut horse nuzzling Katrina a week later.

"He is, isn't he?" Katrina agreed, stroking his face.

"With Faith, too," Jill said. "They're always grazing together now."

"And she always comes and stands near him when I'm dressing his leg," Katrina said. "It's like she wants to help. Having her around seems to calm him down."

"So when do you think you are going to start jumping him?" Josie asked. Ever since Dr. Vaughan had said the bandage could come off, Katrina had been riding Flight a bit more. She had been walking and trotting him around the field but hadn't tried cantering or jumping yet.

"I don't know," Katrina answered. "Dr. Vaughan said he should be fine to jump, but . . ." Her voice trailed off.

"But what?" Jill asked.

Katrina frowned, her eyes troubled. "I'm just worried about it, I guess. I know I've been jumping Faith, but Flight's different. He's so sensitive. I know that if I'm at all scared he'll pick up on it." She shook her head. "I'm not going to rush into it."

"But what about the show?" Josie asked. She hadn't brought up the subject of the horse show at all, because she had not wanted to upset Katrina more, but jumping was Katrina's best event.

"I'm not going to think about that right now," Katrina replied. "I just want to take things one day at a time. If he's ready, we'll go. If he's not, well, we'll stay at home. It's not the end of the world. It's just a show. Flight's being injured has made me realize that there are more important things than shows. As long as he's happy, that's all that matters to me."

Katrina continued to ride Flight lightly all week. On Saturday, she put up a small cross-rail. "He's being so calm I'm going to try to jump him," she said to Jill and Josie as she saddled up. "But I want to warm him up properly. I don't want to jump him until all his muscles are loose and he's ready."

Josie smiled. Katrina had really changed her attitude toward Flight since the accident. Now she always put him first.

After twenty minutes, Flight was working quietly on a long, loose rein. "Well, here goes," Katrina said, as she rode past the fence.

She turned Flight toward the jump. As soon as he saw it, his ears pricked forward and his whole body seemed to stiffen. Tossing his head, he plunged forward.

"Whoa!" Katrina turned him away from the jump in alarm. He fought for his head in excitement. It took three circles before she could slow him down to a trot and finally a walk.

Katrina rode him over to the fence, her face full of disappointment. "It's no good. Look how excited he is. He wants to jump at a flat-out gallop, but if he does that, he might hurt himself."

Josie wished she knew what to suggest. "Try it again," she said. "Maybe it just took him by surprise. After all, you haven't jumped him for a while."

Katrina didn't look convinced, but she rode Flight toward the jump once again. The same thing happened. He tensed and tried to shoot forward.

"No!" Katrina said, turning him away.

Behind them, Faith whinnied. Josie turned. Faith was watching Flight, her eyes following him as he moved toward the fence.

An idea sprang into Josie's mind. "Maybe Faith can help," she suggested, as Katrina rode over to her and Jill. "Perhaps if Jill is in the field with you, it will calm Flight."

"Yes, it might help," said Jill.

"I guess anything's worth a try." Katrina didn't look convinced. While Josie and Jill tacked Faith up, she rode Flight in large circles away from the jump.

"Do you think this is going to work?" Jill asked Josie as she mounted Faith.

"I don't know," Josie admitted in a low tone as she looked at Flight. He had his head up, and his nostrils were flaring. "But it can't make things any worse."

Jill rode Faith to meet Flight. Seeing them come across the field, Flight whinnied shrilly in excitement. Faith kept on walking, her strides steady and her eyes calm. When she reached Flight, her nostrils moved in a soft nicker. Flight instantly seemed to relax.

Katrina glanced at Jill. "Let's just let them walk around together for a few minutes."

They moved off. Flight pranced at first, but gradually he settled down, and soon the two horses were walking around the field together. They moved into a trot and then a canter.

"Faith seems to be calming him down," Josie said as they passed the gate.

"I'm going to try a jump," Katrina said.

"Good luck!" Josie called.

Jill pulled Faith to a halt and watched as they moved toward the jump. Trotting steadily, Flight approached the fence. Three strides away from the jump, he broke into a steady canter, and suddenly he was arcing over it.

"Good boy!" Katrina cried in delight.

"That was great!" Josie exclaimed.

"Do it again!" Jill said eagerly.

Calm now, Flight soared over the fences easily, with room to spare.

As he landed safely after the last fence, Katrina's face wore a grin of delight. "We did it. We're jumping again!"

"He looked fantastic!" Josie cried.

Katrina's eyes sparkled as Flight stopped near Faith. "He was just so relaxed!" Patting him, she looked gratefully at Jill. "Thanks, Jill. Having Faith work with him really calmed him down!"

Faith nuzzled Flight and exhaled noisily. "She says she enjoyed it," Jill laughed.

"That last jump felt so good," Katrina exclaimed. "I've never felt this in control when I've jumped him before. I didn't feel scared at all. I want to jump again and again. Though, since I'm taking things slowly, I'm not going to, of course," she added quickly.

"So does this mean you might take Flight to the show?" Josie asked eagerly. She couldn't contain her excitement anymore.

"If he continues to be this good," Katrina said, "I'll definitely go."

Flight whinnied in agreement.

Josie smiled. "You know, I think he's saying that's just fine by him!"

The three girls looked at each and shared a big smile. The show was going to be fun for all of them!

CHAPTER
TEN

Flight continued to jump well over the next couple of days. Katrina increased the size of the jumps, but she always started with them low and raised the poles only when Flight was fully warmed up.

"Tomorrow's going to be so exciting," said Jill, as she and Josie helped Katrina clean Flight's tack the day before the big show. "I can't wait."

"I know," Josie agreed. "Mom said she'll drive me, Anna, and Ben over to watch."

"Mom, Dad, and I are coming," Jill said. "There'll be loads of people to cheer you on, Katrina."

"I just hope we do well," Katrina said anxiously.

"Flight will be great," Josie told her. "He's jumping so well now—he's so much calmer."

"But that's here, in the field," Katrina fretted. "Is he going to stay calm at the show? What if he gets overexcited being at a show ground again? There's going to be loads of entries. All it would take would be one fence falling, and we'll be out of the competition."

"It's a shame Faith can't come with you," Jill said. "She always seems to calm him down."

Josie stared at her. "That's it!"

Jill and Katrina looked confused.

"Don't you see?" Josie went on excitedly. "That's the answer! You should take Faith to the show with him, Katrina."

Katrina's eyes widened. "I suppose we could. Uncle David is taking us there in my trailer, and it holds two horses. Faith could travel with Flight."

"It's a fabulous idea!" Jill exclaimed.

Katrina jumped to her feet. "I'll go and ask," she said to Jill.

Josie and Jill waited eagerly for her to come back. The plan was perfect!

Katrina came running out of the house. "Uncle David says it's fine! Faith can come!"

"She'll love it!" Jill shouted.

"And hopefully it'll help Flight," Josie said.

Katrina looked as if a weight had been lifted from her shoulders. "It's worth a try."

"You're going to do great!" Josie declared.

"Class number thirty-six, the Barker and Mayne Senior Final, will begin shortly in Ring One," the loudspeaker crackled as Josie jumped out of the car the next day with Anna and Ben.

"That's not Katrina's class, is it?" asked Anna.

"No," Josie told her. "She's in the Regional Final in Ring Two."

"Wow! This is a huge show!" exclaimed Ben, looking around at the five rings, the rows of horse trailers, and the covered stands selling everything one could possibly want for a horse.

Josie nodded. There were people everywhere—riders working on beautiful horses in gleaming tack, stable hands carrying grooming boxes, riding instructors shouting advice, and parents hurrying across the grass, looking confused.

"Should we go and find the Atterburys?" Mrs. Grace asked.

"Definitely," Josie replied. All the way to the show she had been thinking about Katrina and Flight.

They headed toward the horse trailers.

"How are we going to find them?" Ben said. "There are tons of horses here."

"Let's start at one end and work our way down," Mary Grace suggested.

But just as they had started to walk past the first row of trailers, Josie saw two familiar figures in the distance. "There's Katrina and Jill!" she exclaimed. "Katrina! Jill!"

Katrina and Jill looked around.

"Hey!" Katrina called back.

"We were just looking for you," Anna told them. "Katrina, this is my brother, Ben." The two said hello.

"We were beginning to wonder if we would ever find you," Josie said.

"The trailer's over there. Flight and Faith are tied up outside," Katrina explained. "Uncle David and Aunt Jane went to get some water. I've been walking the course with Jill."

"The jumps are huge!" Jill said.

"How's Flight?" Josie asked as they began to follow Katrina through the trailers.

"Excited, but not too wild," Katrina answered. She pointed ahead. "Look, there he is."

Josie looked. Flight and Faith were tied up to the outside of Katrina's trailer. Faith was pulling calmly at a hay net. Flight was looking around with his ears pricked forward, but he didn't seem agitated, just interested in everything that was going on.

"Your idea is working, Josie," said Katrina. "He's much calmer than he usually is at a show. Having Faith here really seems to have made a difference."

Hearing her voice, Flight looked around and whinnied.

Katrina stopped in her tracks. "He whinnied at me!" She hurried forward. "Hey, boy." She gently patted Flight's neck, as he nuzzled her hands.

Katrina glanced at the others. "He actually whinnied at me." She sounded as though she couldn't believe it.

Mrs. Grace's face became thoughtful. "You know, maybe his calmness isn't just because of Faith, Katrina. Maybe it's because of you."

"What do you mean?" Katrina asked.

"Well, since the accident you've been spending a lot more time with him," Mrs. Grace replied. "I think he's started to bond with you, and that that's why he's becoming calmer. I mean, I'm sure having Faith here is helping," she added, going over and stroking Faith's bay neck. "But I think the most important change is that he's discovered that he can rely on you."

Katrina stared at her. "Really?"

"Really," said Mrs. Grace. "He knows that if he's in trouble, you'll come through for him. That's calmed him down. You've earned his trust, and that's everything. Now a real partnership can start between you—if you want it."

"I do," Katrina said, stroking Flight's nose. "I really do! Over the last few weeks, I've realized that I don't want to just ride him anymore. I want to take care of him and have him love me, as Charity loves you, Josie, and as Faith loves Jill."

"He will," Mrs. Grace said softly.

Katrina smiled at Josie. "This has turned out to be some summer vacation."

Josie smiled back.

There was a buzzing from the sound system, and the show announcer's voice crackled out of a nearby speaker. "Class forty-one, the Regional Final, is now starting in Ring Two."

"That's my class!" Katrina said. "I'm not jumping till the end, but I'd better start warming him up, anyway."

"I'll tack him up for you while you get changed," said Jill.

"I'll help!" Ann and Ben offered at once.

"Me, too!" Josie said.

An hour later, Katrina cantered Flight into the ring. His hooves glistened with hoof oil, and his tail floated out behind him. Katrina looked great in tan breeches and a navy show jacket. She patted Flight's shining neck and brought him to a halt to salute the judges. As she pushed him into a canter again, she glanced to the side, where Josie, Jill, Anna, and Ben were watching, along with Mrs. Grace and Mr. and Mrs. Atterbury.

Anna clutched Josie's arm. "I hope he jumps clear."

Josie nodded. Her heart was thumping. There had

been eleven clear rounds already. For Katrina to get into the jump-off and stand a chance of qualifying for the national final, Flight could not afford to make a single mistake. "Go on, Flight," Josie whispered, as Flight turned toward the first jump.

She needn't have worried. He flew over it.

"Awesome!" Ben exclaimed as Flight soared over the next jump, an imposing red wall.

"He's perfect!" Anna agreed. "And Katrina's an amazing rider!"

Josie watched wordlessly, her body feeling as though it were moving in time with Flight's. She had never seen him look that good. He was calm and in control. His ears were pricked up, and he really seemed to be listening to his rider. Sitting effortlessly in the saddle, Katrina guided him over the eight jumps. *Please go clear, please go clear.* The words went around and around in Josie's head.

As Flight cleared the last fence, Josie jumped up. "Yes!" she exclaimed in delight.

"They did it!" Jill shouted.

Josie hugged Anna. "They went clear!" they both cried.

Around them, the crowd clapped loudly. Letting

go of each other, Anna and Josie joined in with Jill and Ben's cheers as Katrina rode past. She was grinning and patting Flight over and over again.

"She rode him beautifully!" Mrs. Grace said.

"Come on, let's hurry and go find her!" Anna exclaimed. They hurried along the stands and out onto the grass. But as they came within view of Katrina and Flight, they realized that they had been beaten to the punch. A man and a woman were standing beside Flight. Katrina had gotten off her horse and was hugging them.

"It's her mom and dad!" Josie exclaimed, recognizing the couple that had brought Katrina and Flight to Jill's house.

"Aunt Rachel and Uncle Andrew!" Jill cried, in shock. "They must have gotten back early."

They all ran over to the group.

When she saw them, Katrina broke away from her parents. "Mom and Dad got here just in time!" Her eyes shone happily. "They saw my round."

"We thought we were going to miss it, but we got to the ring as Katrina was going in," Katrina's mom said, as Jill's parents and Mrs. Grace came to join them. "We caught an earlier flight home."

"Didn't she do well?" Mr. Atterbury said.

"Flight was fantastic!" Katrina said, hugging her horse's damp neck.

Josie grinned at her. "And now you've just got to do it all again in the jump-off!"

rounds before his, but Flight flew around all the jumps, cutting every corner and finishing three seconds faster than the lead horse.

He was the last horse in the jump-off, and as he crossed the finish line and the clock stopped, Josie, Anna, Ben, and Jill went wild.

"They won!" Josie shouted excitedly.

"They're in the national final!" Jill exclaimed, hugging Faith, whom she had brought to the ring with her.

"Hooray!" Anna and Ben yelled.

Even the grown-ups seemed caught up in the excitement. They clapped and cheered as Katrina rode past, a huge grin on her face.

The steward told her to stay in the ring, and the other five riders who had placed were called in to join her. Lining up in a row, they were presented with certificates, beautiful four-tier ribbons, and envelopes containing prize money.

As Katrina received her ribbon, she looked over toward Josie and Jill. *Thank you,* she mouthed, and smiled.

"The winners will now canter a victory l— the announcer.

Katrina leaned forward, and right moved into a smooth canter. Jill turned to Josie with a smile. "Isn't it wonderful?" she asked above the clapping and cheering. "Imagine being Katrina now."

Josie grinned. "The way you're going with your jumping, it could be you. A huge log today, a show-jumping arena tomorrow . . ."

"No," Jill replied, shaking her head. "I mean, it's really exciting for Katrina, but I don't want it." She kissed Faith happily. "Having Faith to ride and love is good enough for me!"